The _____ _____
undeniable _____

He pushed through the small gathering and stood before her.

"Are you all right?"

Jessica must have bumped her head harder than she thought. She felt suddenly paralyzed, as if she couldn't breathe. "I'm f-f-fine," she managed to stammer.

"Jessica King?"

"How did you know?"

"Lucky guess." Did she detect dryness in his tone? He scowled and, without warning, touched the corner of her lip.

Intellectually, Jessica supposed she had known life could change—completely, irrevocably, permanently—in a split second. She supposed she had always had a peripheral awareness that fate and the most well-planned of lives were sometimes on a collision course. What she had not believed was that something as innocuous as a chance meeting, a rough finger laid on the delicate skin of her upper lip, could bring on this sensation.

That everything about her reasonable and well-ordered life had just changed.

Dear Reader,

After looking at winter's bleak landscape and feeling her icy cold breezes, I found nothing to be more rewarding than savoring the warm ocean breezes from a poolside lounge chair as I read a soon-to-be favorite book or two! Of course, as I choose my books for this long-anticipated outing, this month's Silhouette Romance offerings will be on the top of my pile.

Cara Colter begins the month with *Chasing Dreams* (#1818), part of her A FATHER'S WISH trilogy. In this poignant title, a beautiful academic moves outside her comfort zone and feels alive for the first time in the arms of a brawny man who would seem her polar opposite. When an unexpected night of passion results in a pregnancy, the hero and heroine learn that duty can bring its own sweet rewards, in *Wishing and Hoping* (#1819), the debut book in beloved series author Susan Meier's THE CUPID CAMPAIGN miniseries. Elizabeth Harbison sets out to discover whether bustling New York City will prove the setting for a modern-day fairy tale when an ordinary woman comes face-to-face with one of the world's most eligible royals, in *If the Slipper Fits* (#1820). Finally, Lissa Manley rounds out the month with *The Parent Trap* (#1821), in which two matchmaking girls set out to invent a family.

Be sure to return next month when Cara Colter concludes her heartwarming trilogy.

Happy reading!

Ann Leslie Tuttle
Associate Senior Editor

Please address questions and book requests to:
Silhouette Reader Service
U.S.: 3010 Walden Ave., P.O. Box 1325, Buffalo, NY 14269
Canadian: P.O. Box 609, Fort Erie, Ont. L2A 5X3

CARA COLTER

CHASING DREAMS

A Father's Wish

SILHOUETTE *Romance* ®

Published by Silhouette Books

America's Publisher of Contemporary Romance

With special thanks to Pamela Elliott of Walt's Auto Service for answering all my questions with patience, good humor and professionalism.

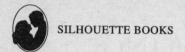 SILHOUETTE BOOKS

ISBN 0-373-19818-3

CHASING DREAMS

Copyright © 2006 by Cara Colter

Books by Cara Colter

Silhouette Romance

Dare To Dream #491
Baby in Blue #1161
Husband in Red #1243
*The Cowboy, the Baby
   and the Bride-To-Be* #1319
Truly Daddy #1363
A Bride Worth Waiting For #1388
Weddings Do Come True #1406
A Babe in the Woods #1424
A Royal Marriage #1440
First Time, Forever #1464
Husband by Inheritance #1532
The Heiress Takes a Husband #1538
Wed by a Will #1544

What Child Is This? #1585
Her Royal Husband #1600
*9 Out of 10 Women Can't Be
   Wrong* #1615
*Guess Who's Coming for
   Christmas?* #1632
What a Woman Should Know
   #1685
Major Daddy #1710
Her Second-Chance Man #1726
Nighttime Sweethearts #1754
†*That Old Feeling* #1814
†*Chasing Dreams* #1818

Silhouette Books

The Coltons
A Hasty Wedding
*The Wedding Legacy
†A Father's Wish

CARA COLTER

shares ten acres in the wild Kootenay region of British Columbia with the man of her dreams, three children, two horses, a cat with no tail and a golden retriever who answers best to "bad dog." She loves reading, writing and the woods in winter (no bears). She says life's delights include an automatic garage door opener and the skylight over the bed that allows her to see the stars at night. She also says, "I have not lived a neat and tidy life, and used to envy those who did. Now I see my struggles as having given me a deep appreciation of life, and of love, that I hope I succeed in passing on through the stories that I tell."

A Mechanic's Guide to Love and Restoring Classic Cars:

1. Start with good "bones"; what's beneath the surface is what makes a car—and a woman—beautiful

2. Be patient

3. Be persistent

4. Do your homework so you'll know what you are working with

5. Trust that what is and what can be are only separated by desire, determination and a little bit of help from fate

Prologue

"That insolent young pup!" Jake King slammed down the phone. He was eighty-three years old, he was one of the wealthiest and most respected businessmen in America and he was dying. He had a right to have his wishes granted!

They were simple wishes: happy marriages for the three daughters born to him so late in his life and a perfectly refurbished 1923 Rolls-Royce Silver Ghost Oxford Open Tourer for himself.

Things had been going rather well in the wish department. Just last weekend he had attended the wedding of his oldest daughter, twenty-six-year-old Brandgwen, to one of his most cherished business associates. The happiness and love shining in Brandy's eyes—just the way he had planned it—had made Jake overly confident. It had made him think he could have whatever he wanted, that God granted wishes to dying men.

Or maybe acquiring the Rolls had seemed like less of a challenge than trying to save his middle daughter, Jessica, from herself.

Jake sighed. Jessica announcing her engagement to Professor Mitch Michaels at Brandy's wedding had put a black spot on the whole event.

A black spot on his life.

Possibly he was trying to erase it with the Rolls.

He glared at the picture of the car on the Internet, and particularly at the disgustingly handsome young man who leaned beside it, grinning confidently, dark hair falling over eyes so like his grandfather's had been. Dark, snapping with defiance.

"I should have known he wouldn't sell me the car," Jake muttered. There was bad blood between the Blakes and the Kings. It hadn't always been that way. No, far from it. That insolent young pup's grandfather, Simon, had been Jake's business partner, way before the phenomenal success story of Auto Kingdom. And it might have remained that way, if Simon's son, Billy, hadn't been such an arrogant ne'er-do-well.

Billy would have sold him the car, Jake thought cynically. He would have sold it in a flash, just like he had sold everything else. But the grandson was a different story. Inner toughness shone from his eyes.

Garner Blake had made something of himself, despite the horrendous debts he'd inherited as a result of his father's runaway grandiosity. It seemed Garner shared his grandfather's passion for cars. He brought old beauties back to life. He did it better than anyone else in the business.

Jake knew these things. A man was smart to keep track of his enemies.

The door to his office burst open, and his assistant, Sarah, came in with his new son-in-law's baby, Becky, riding on her hip. Becky was staying at Kingsway while her dad and new mommy honeymooned.

"Do you want to go see Grandpa Jake?" she asked the child.

The baby's weight settled against him, and he allowed himself to appreciate the miracle and the marvel of her. When he had found out he was dying he had wished for a grandchild. For happiness for his daughters. He had wished he could show them, somehow, that only one thing really mattered.

Love.

Okay, love and good cars, but mostly love.

He had succeeded with his eldest daughter, succeeded beyond his wildest dreams at his first awkward attempt at matchmaking.

But Jessie, his second daughter, was different. Jessie was disconnected and intellectual. Given those defects, Mitch Michaels was simply unsuitable. The good professor, while obviously an honorable and stable man, could only bring out those qualities in her. Her beauty would remain forever hidden under layers of prim control that Mitch actually seemed to encourage.

Poor Jessie. The girl was twenty-four years old. She had no business acting so old. She always seemed to have her head down, in a book. She needed a man who could show her how to look up, dream a little, touch the sky.

He mulled over the surprising poetry of those thoughts while the baby pulled at his nose and his ears.

Really, especially after his episode with the Blake lad, it was beginning to feel like too much for him. What did he know of poetry and passion? Where could he find such things for his daughter? His energy was waning, his light dimming, and so much more quickly than he had expected.

"Look what I found," Sarah said. She looked like Brandy. And sometimes there was a lilt in her voice that reminded him of a time long ago.

She plunked a picture down in front of him. Over the objections of his secretary, James, and just about everybody else in this household, he had given Sarah a job. She was sorting through mountains of photos and assembling memory albums, one for each of his daughters. Sarah was good at it, and he was glad he had hired her to put together a suitable memento for the daughters who had no idea that soon they would be looking at their father only in picture albums.

"I didn't quite know what to make of it."

Jake studied what she had placed before him. It was an old photo, sepia, the edges curling. It was a picture of himself as a young man, his arm looped casually around the shoulders of his best friend, Simon Blake. Jake felt a slight tremble in his hand. How odd that he had just hung up on Garner Blake and now this picture would be presented to him.

Or perhaps not odd at all… The veil between the worlds of the seen and the unseen were thinning. Perhaps all things were linked in ways he had never allowed himself to believe before.

He studied the photo of the two happy young men. Behind them, draped in a grand opening banner, was a building that couldn't have possibly been big enough to hold all their youthful hopes and dreams. K & B Auto, the humble beginning of the Auto Kingdom empire in Farewell, Virginia.

And the beginning of the end of something far more precious than all the successes he had ever enjoyed.

The beginning of the end of his lifelong friendship with Simon. Not Simon's fault. Simon's son, Billy's. Billy had managed to squander every single thing his father had worked for. In the end, Billy owned only his half of that small shop. No doubt he would have lost that, too, had Jake ever been willing to sell his share.

Jake felt the sharpness of regret.

Had he been too hard on Simon's son? Probably. It was not until he had children of his own, long after Billy had grown, that he understood the complete helplessness of that love, the compulsion to overindulge.

He recalled his conversation with Garner. Hadn't he heard the stamp of Simon's own resolve in that young man's strong, confident voice? Yes. And he'd heard more. A fierceness of spirit that reminded him of who he himself, Jake King, had once been. Plus, that love of cars, passed to Garner straight from Simon.

Jessie's love of cars remained, too, under all that intellectual frou-frou.

Jessie and Simon's grandson. Was it possible? Could Jake repair his mistakes of the past and manipulate his daughter's future in one fell swoop? A shiver traveled the length of his spine.

Perhaps the gods would take pity on a man with so much to do, and so little time left. He snorted. This kind of thought had to be contained, or next he would be consulting his daily horoscope and reading crystals to find direction.

Of course, where he was going, who was to say where the direction would come from? Perhaps hunch and instinct and all those nebulous things came from heaven's door. Meanwhile, he had a lot of homework to do on Mr. Garner Blake before Jake would cross the young man's path with that of his beloved Jessie.

Reluctantly, he passed the baby back to Sarah. "Tell James I need to talk to Cameron McPherson, at once."

Did she color at the mention of that name? Ah, yes, he recalled. She had danced with Cameron at the wedding. He saw the longing flash through her eyes. Too bad it wouldn't be so easy with Jessie.

Three days later, with a thick folder in front of him, Jake redialed that number in Farewell, Virginia. He knew everything there was to know about Garner Blake. And he liked what he had found out. Garner was tough, but innately decent. What was best about his grandfather had survived in him. He had been nominated Citizen of the Year by the town of Farewell, and Jake's sources told him Blake would win.

He let none of what he was feeling—excitement and hope—show in his voice. Instead, Jake King informed Garner Blake, coldly, that his daughter would be coming to work at K & B Auto for the summer, to fill the long-vacant position of office manager.

"Have you been spying on me?" Garner asked, his voice hard and incredulous.

Jake chose not to answer. Instead, he reminded Garner that he owned half the business and was, according to the legal documents he was looking at, entitled to hire and fire employees.

There was the faintest veiled threat in his statement. He knew from the dossier in front of him that Garner Blake hired good men to work for him and he was intensely loyal to each of them. Jake also knew one of those men had just had a baby, another had just bought a home. They were men who needed their jobs.

There was a long silence on the other end of the line.

Then Garner said, "Is this about the car?"

"If it was, would you change your mind?"

"No."

"That's what I thought."

Jake hung up the phone thoughtfully. He hadn't broken it to Jessie that he'd found her a summer job. He had a feeling she wasn't going to be any happier about the arrangement than Garner Blake was.

She had just completed a master's degree in science and she was contemplating beginning her Ph.D. She was brilliant and academically successful and she wasn't going to want to work the front counter of an auto repair shop.

She could refuse. But he doubted she would. If he was dealing with her younger sister, Chelsea, he would have to threaten the trust fund, the allowance, the car and the credit cards. But Jessie was not Chelsea. She had always wanted to please him. He recalled, affectionately, the soft worry in her green eyes when she looked at him, even as a child.

Despite his treachery in playing with his unsuspecting daughter's well-ordered life, he decided to call her immediately and smiled when he heard her voice on the other end of the phone. It was all for the greater good, after all.

Chapter One

The wedding gown was designed by Dior. The bride was slender and radiant. Her bouquet held pure white French Lace floribunda roses, flown in from Oregon.

The groom waited at the end of the aisle. He was turning toward her—

The daydream ended with a *bang*. Literally.

Jessica King's head flew forward and hit the steering wheel. After a stunned moment, she stared at the crumpled hood of the car she had rented earlier this morning after flying into Harrisonburg, Virginia. Beyond the damaged front of the car was the parking meter she had hit, and beyond that was the rather dingy cream stucco storefront of K & B Auto.

Steam hissed out of the hood of her damaged Cadillac, and a small crowd began to gather.

"That's what dreaming will get you," Jessie admonished herself.

Embarrassed rather than hurt, Jessie took a deep breath and stepped from the car. Emerging from the air-conditioning into the steamy heat of an early-summer morning took her by surprise. But not as much as being watched by half a dozen or so people, their interest in her unabashed. There was really nothing she hated quite so much as being the center of attention.

Odd then that she had been imagining her wedding day instead of paying attention to what she was doing. Was there a day where a person was more the center of attention than that one? Of the King girls, she was the practical one, the pragmatic one, the nondreamer.

"For good reason," she muttered, surveying the damage to the car. It had been a beautiful car, undeserving of her carelessness.

She was not a careless person! Not the least ditzy! And yet, after overcoming her initial surprise at Mitch's announcement of their engagement at her sister's wedding only two weeks ago, she was astonished to find a romantic hidden within herself, a romantic who simply could not get enough of daydreaming about every detail of her big day.

"I'm sorry," she mumbled to the onlookers. "I just didn't see the meter. Over the hood. I don't usually drive a car with such a large hood..."

Her voice trailed off as the front door of K & B Auto swung open and a man emerged.

The last residue of her wedding fantasy faded.

Her entire former life faded.

The man had huge and undeniable presence. He was big, six feet or better, and every inch of that frame was muscular and spare. She could see power in every line of him, from the way his faded jeans clung to the large muscles in his thigh to the way the short-sleeved white T-shirt hugged the hard curve of a bicep and the washboard smoothness of his stomach. His hair was as dark as devil's food cake, a little too long at the collar. His facial features were clean and chiseled, but the hardness in the line of his body was repeated in the stamp of his face—in the faint whisker-roughness of cheekbones and chin, in dark slashes of brows arrowing downward, in the line of lips that appeared stern and forbidding. How was it that the fullness of those lips made him sensual in a way that overrode his obvious ill temper? His eyes were animal dark, brown bordering on black, and a light snapped in them that was fierce, frightening, compelling.

He pushed through the small gathering and stood before her.

"Are you all right?"

She must have bumped her head harder than she originally thought. It was only four small words grouped together to form a question, and there was no sincere compassion in that question, either. In fact, the man seemed to be bristling with impatience. And yet she felt suddenly paralyzed, as if she couldn't breathe.

"I'm f-f-fine," she managed to stammer.

"Jessica King?" His gravel-edged voice scraped across the delicate skin at the back of her neck like a physical touch.

"How did you know?"

"Lucky guess," he said. Did she detect a certain dryness to his tone? Then his scowl deepened. Without warning he reached out and touched the corner of her lip.

Intellectually, Jessica King supposed she had known life could change—completely, irrevocably, permanently—in a split second. She supposed she had always had a peripheral awareness that fate and the most well-planned lives were sometimes on a collision course. She had heard about such things: the decision to fly instead of to drive, a right-hand turn instead of a left one, and *poof*, a life changed for all time. What she had not believed was that something as innocuous as a chance meeting, a rough finger laid on the delicate skin of her upper lip, could bring on this sensation, not unlike drowning, that everything about her reasonable and well-ordered world had just changed.

What she had not believed was that such a thing could ever happen to her.

Lives forever altered by chance, by the whimsy of the gods, happened to other people, perhaps to people more spontaneous than she was or those more willing to take chances. She had lived with the happy illusion that fate had a much better chance of toying with people less organized, less in control, less dedicated to routine and precision than Jessica King.

His finger left her lip, and she returned to her well-ordered world with a *pop,* though she could not quite shake the sensation that there might remain a scorch mark where he had touched.

The devil will do that, she told herself. And the man was a devil, so at ease in his body, radiating self-assuredness. He had a roguish, untamed quality that was damnably sexy.

And he was no doubt exactly like every other man who was damnably sexy. He would know it and play it.

Jessica King would not be like her deceased, and rather infamous, mother. Not ever. She despised women who were helpless against the raw power that radiated from certain kinds of men.

This kind of man.

"Keep your mucky fingers to yourself," she said, bristling with annoyance. He had come out of K & B Auto, likely a mechanic. His fingers would, of course, be mucky. Her eyes trailed to his hand. A big hand, the knuckles grazed, the back corded with a powerful network of vein and sinew. No ring. No muck.

He seemed unmoved by her annoyance, if he'd even had the good manners to notice it. Instead, he was studying the finger that had touched her lip. She noted, stiffly, it appeared to have *muck* on it.

"I thought it was blood on your lip," he said. "But it's not, is it?"

His eyes met hers, and a hint of laughter overrode his bad temper. Then he grinned, a small gesture, a tilting of firm lips. The grin changed everything. It was the sun glimpsed in the midst of a storm. The warrior cast of the face was momentarily transformed and he looked young and boyish and even more irresistible than he had before.

She shook her head. Now that was the *real* world. Men like this laughed at girls like her, girls who wore glasses and never got their hair quite right and were a teensy bit overweight. Never mind that the brief spark of laughter lighting the darkness of his eyes was more seductive than...

"Chocolate," he said, and a small ripple of laughter went through the crowd, which was beginning to drift away now that the car was evidently just going to sit there hissing and not blow up.

He didn't join in the laughter, and she was sorry he wasn't having a laugh at her expense. A good defense against a man like him would be pure, unadulterated hatred.

"And you are?" she demanded. She resisted an impulse to tug at her skirt, which suddenly seemed binding around her hips.

How much weight had she gained since her sister's wedding? Seven and a half pounds, as if she didn't know *exactly*. You would think a person would have to work at gaining that much weight in such a short period of time, but she had no idea how—

"Garner Blake."

She closed her eyes, just briefly, praying for strength. *This* was the man she was going to be working for?

"Oh, no." It slipped out.

"My sentiments exactly," he said.

She opened her eyes and glared at him. "Then why am I here?"

"Because your father wanted you to be. And for the most part, it would seem that what Jake King wants, Jake King gets."

That *for the most part* seemed loaded with satisfaction.

Her father had told her that he was part owner in an obscure little business called K & B Auto that needed an office manager for the summer. He had told her he wanted her to get a taste of the real world.

Of course, she'd been briefly offended that he didn't think her world was real and that he did not understand she was rather overqualified to be an office manager. She would have said so, too, except she had heard something in his voice that had troubled her. His voice had lacked strength, and the tone of his words had been faintly pleading.

Her father had never asked anything of her. So many times she had wished he would. When her father had asked this of her, she had sensed there was history here, a story, perhaps even a secret, that went beyond the fact that this humble little garage in nowhere Virginia was where it had all started for him. Her logical mind had known she needed more details, but for once logic had fled her. Looking at the predicament she was in now, it had probably been an omen.

When she should have been asking important questions, all she had been thinking was finally her father had recognized her. Finally he was seeing, even in the smallest way, that she was an educated woman of sound business skill, not one of his little princesses. She had assumed he was trusting her with a business assignment for Auto Kingdom!

"You do need an office manager, don't you?" she asked, and was annoyed to hear a little tremor of uncertainty in her voice.

He must have heard it, too, because he sighed, pushed a large, impatient hand through tousled locks and made an obvious effort to restrain his impatience.

"Lady, I am absolutely desperate for an office manager. It's just that the job requires a little know-how. The type of training you don't get at the debutante ball or out fox hunting with the hounds."

She felt herself stiffen. As if she hadn't been up against this kind of prejudice her whole life.

"You might be interested to know I've never attended a debutante ball," she said sharply, "and I don't ride horses." *Terrified of them, actually,* though she was reluctant to admit weakness to this man.

Chelsea did the balls. Brandy did the horses. Had he mixed her up with one of her sisters?

"You get my drift," he said.

Oh, yes, she did. Useless. Rich. Frivolous.

"I happen to have a master's degree," she said tightly.

She decided now might not be the best time to mention it was in science. Still, she was confident that anybody who could spend two years painstakingly researching and documenting the effects of pesticides on the bone structure of prairie dogs, as she had just done, could handle a little office work.

He looked at her narrowly, his gaze so long and so stripping that she had to disguise a tiny tremor of…something.

"A master's degree," he repeated slowly. "Okay, that's a surprise."

"Didn't my father tell you anything about me?"

"No. And I didn't ask."

She was struck with a sensation that she had been dropped in the middle of a war zone, completely unarmed.

"You might as well come and see what you've gotten yourself into." Again, she heard a hard note of satisfaction in his voice.

He turned and walked away from her, not even waiting to see if she would follow.

Used to having women follow him like puppies?

Not this woman!

"What about my car?" she asked.

He glanced back at her. "You picked a good place to crash it. Kind of like having a heart attack while visiting the hospital. I'll limp it around to the service bay and have a look at it."

Feeling somehow chastened by his offhand courtesy, she followed him inside. Going from sunlight to indoors, Jessie tried to get her bearings.

Her eyes adjusted and she saw the shop was as humble inside as it had been outside. There was no decor. The floor was black and white linoleum tile, the white squares long since gone to gray. A glass-fronted counter separated the work area from the customer waiting area. The case contained several models of old cars, a faded placard that announced the oil and filter change special and a sample container of the brand of oil that was presumably on sale. Both areas, waiting and work, contained old kitchen chairs, the gray-vinyl padded seats patched with black swatches of tape. The walls held an assortment of calendars, which featured cars, cars and more cars, but thankfully no nude or near-nude women.

The nicest thing about the entire space was a huge picture window that looked onto the main street of Farewell. The morning mist was lifting, and she could see K & B faced the town square—a lovely little park surrounded by a wrought iron fence. It contained several mature trees, green grass, two benches that faced each other and a fountain. In the near distance the mountains looked cool, green and mysterious.

But by the looks of things, she wasn't going to be spending much time admiring the view. Every single surface had papers sliding off of them. There were boxes on the floor with yet more papers and what appeared to be stacks of car parts.

"I think there's been some kind of mistake," she said. The place was a dump. And depressing. The computer was at least a thousand years old. Somehow, even when confronted with the rather dingy exterior of the place, she had imagined she would be running a sleek, state-of-the-art office. She had talked herself into thinking it might be a tiny bit *fun*.

The phone, which was ringing incessantly, looked like an antique. Black, rotary dial. The red light of the answering machine was blinking furiously. From a door that connected the office to the service bays she heard clanking.

"A mistake," she repeated. Jessica King did not do well with chaos.

It was a far cry from the neat little office she had set up in her apartment, from the order of classrooms, from the quiet of fieldwork....

"A mistake," he agreed with silky satisfaction, folding his arms over the ridiculous breadth of his chest and looking at her, pleased that she had lived up to his every unspoken judgment: rich, useless, frivolous *and* chased away by the slightest hint of a challenge.

In less than ten seconds, too!

Jessie was compelled to wipe the smirk off his face, even if it meant she closed the escape door. She straightened her shoulders and tilted her chin.

"Oh, I'm not going anywhere," she said, though of course a split second ago that had been exactly her intent, to cut and run. Aware he was watching her with every ounce of his ill humor returned, she looked for a place to set her purse. She found a tiny corner of clear floor under the desk. Her skirt tightened uncomfortably across her derriere when she bent over, and she straightened hurriedly.

"My specialty is disasters," she said, with cocky confidence that she was far from feeling. "I can fix a mistake like this one—" she motioned to the office with her hand "—in a week."

"A week," he muttered dubiously, and then brightened marginally as he watched her. "Honey, if you last half a day, I'll eat my shorts."

"Briefs or boxers?" she asked. And then she added quickly, "And don't call me *honey*. It's tacky."

"Tacky," he repeated, stunned, as if one of those precariously leaning boxes had slid off the counter and landed on his toe. Thankfully, he focused on the *tacky* enough that he didn't even appear to notice how uncomfortable she was with the uncharacteristically bold remark she had made. Talk about tacky—how about discussing a man's underwear preference?

"Is there any particular part of this mess you'd like cleaned up first?" she said, eager to shift the focus completely.

They were faced off, and she could see she was somewhat of a surprise to him and not an altogether pleasant one, either.

Oh, why hadn't she just turned around and walked back out the door while she still had the chance? Oh, no, Little Miss Has-To-Prove-Herself had to pick the worst moment to put in an appearance.

"Miss King, MBA, that's entirely up to you."

She should really correct him. She had never said a thing about an MBA. "Good," she said decisively. "I'll begin with—"

"No, wait. On second thought, coffee would be a good place to start."

"Coffee," she repeated uneasily. She was pretty sure affirmative action meant that she didn't have to make coffee.

He regarded her rebellious expression cynically, then shook his head.

Something snapped loudly in the vicinity of her desk, and she started, turned and saw nothing. Still, she knew the startle reflex had given away her wee bit of nervousness.

He hadn't missed it. He smiled grimly. "I'm downgrading. Two hours. That's how long you'll make it."

"I hope they're boxers," she shot back. "Those would take you a little longer to eat."

Good grief, this had to stop! She'd known this man less than ten minutes and *she* had mentioned his undergarments twice! She and Mitch had never discussed undergarments, ever.

"And just for future reference, for your next job, in the real world work starts at seven, not—" he glanced at his watch "—eight forty-five."

She wanted to defend herself. Not everyone came in from Harrisonburg, either! But she sensed under these circumstances that excuses, even very legitimate ones, would be wasted.

He picked up a sheaf of papers from a leaning stack on the counter, looked at her once more, shook his head ruefully and headed for the door. The phone started ringing again, and he moved to pick it up, then stopped.

He grinned at her, that grin that made her heart do traitorous and treacherous things. She was glad she was engaged to a man who did not make her feel so topsy-turvy. It would be exhausting to feel this way all the time!

"Hey," he said, his deep voice edged with just a trace of sarcasm, "that would be your job now."

The door shut behind him, and thankfully he took all his bristling energy with him, though without him in it, the room seemed even more depressing than before, if that was possible.

She went around to the other side of the desk, closed her eyes, tried to concentrate. Surely she must have hit her head harder than she thought. She felt shell-shocked, but she took a deep breath, picked up the phone and said, "K & B Auto."

She had barely gotten it out when she was assaulted

by a description of a malfunctioning carburetor in an accent so deep it was nearly indecipherable.

She loved cars. She always had. She loved how they looked and how they smelled and how they sounded when they were running perfectly. She realized what she loved was the *cosmetics* of cars, because she was not even entirely sure what a carburetor was. Maybe she had been a little overly confident in telling that annoying man she was going to bring calm to chaos. She wasn't sure how her master's degree was going to help her with this challenge.

"Call back. Later. Tomorrow would be good." She hung up the phone and sank into a padded leather chair in front of a scarred metal desk overflowing with paper.

The connecting door to the work bay swung open.

"That coffee? I like it strong."

He was zipping himself—very unselfconsciously—into a pair of faded blue coveralls, the jeans and white T-shirt underneath.

The politically correct reply would have been to tell him to make his own damn coffee, but her eyes were mutinously glued to that zipper.

The door shut again before she came to her senses enough to become politically correct.

Coffee. Strong. Now would really be the time to march into the dark cavern of the auto repair bays to tell him he had obviously mistaken her for someone she was not. She *might* be able to manage an office. But girl Friday? Really that was beneath her dignity! She hadn't spent the last six years of her life at school so that she could make coffee and fetch doughnuts!

What on earth had her father been thinking? It was totally evident she was going to be a fish out of water in this environment. It was totally evident this had been a mistake.

"My specialty is disasters," she said, mimicking herself. "I can fix a mistake like this one—in a week."

She pushed back several leaning stacks of paper to make enough room for her elbows. Then she rested her head in her hands and ordered herself to think. Thinking was generally her specialty, not that she had let even a hint of that show in the encounter she had just survived. Nor was any of her natural intelligence surfacing now. Because instead of formulating a plan of attack for the terrible mess in this office, and the huge coffee machine that gloated at her from its perch on the crowded counter, she was lamenting her choice of outfit.

A terrible choice. A suit, classic Chanel, jacket and straight skirt, in a small plaid pattern that had made her feel exceedingly professional when she had chosen it, along with dark stockings and plain black pumps, this morning. It was the type of outfit her fiancé, Mitch, approved of. Respectable. Mature. Appropriate for someone planning an academic career.

It makes you look fat, a voice inside her head wailed. Plus, it was going to be too hot. Her office space already seemed sauna-like, though in fairness, part of that might be her reaction to Garner Blake.

And her hair! Why had she ever allowed her sister Chelsea to talk her into cutting it? Oh, because Chelsea had talked about bone structure and her eyes and had made her believe, somehow, that having only two inches of hair could make her other features seem extraordinary!

Of course, under Chelsea's hand—that wheat-blond hair coaxed into a riot of cheerful curls—that had happened. For Brandy's wedding, Chelsea had also used makeup like an artist used a brush. In moments, Jessie had found herself in possession of startling cheekbones, stunning eyes, a sinfully puffy bottom lip.

But left to her own devices? Jessie felt her new "do" managed to look like she had slept with a demon-possessed rolling pin. Desperate for some semblance of order from her unruly hair she had taken to wetting it down, plastering it against her head and letting it dry like that. Without looking in a mirror, she knew the result was less than stellar, a drowned rat mixed with a hel-met-head kind of look.

And makeup? A tiny line of gloss around her lips, a hint of mascara, a touch of blush. The result? *Dull. Dull. Dull.*

Stop it, Jessie commanded herself. The order of business was not to sit here wishing for another oppor-tunity to make that all-important first impression. If she had it to do again, she should not waste her wishes on beauty. Why should she care if Garner Blake thought she was attractive? She was already taken, engaged, not available for the man-woman game anymore. She was relieved about that. The rules and procedures had always seemed just a little nebulous. She was a disaster at inter-changes with the opposite sex, and she was darned lucky to have found Mitch, who appreciated her for her mind.

No, if she was throwing wishes around, she should opt for a chance to look brilliant.

Just a year from her doctoral degree, if she chose to continue her prairie dog study, and she had managed to present herself as a complete imbecile from the moment she had stepped out of her smoking car.

She had confidently proclaimed her master's degree qualified her to look after his office, and she could clearly see it would take something much more than that.

"A combination of the Queen of Clean and Trump," she muttered out loud.

Sitting at this horribly messy desk in a building that smelled of grease and other mysterious and extremely masculine substances, and that was heating up more by the second, it occurred to her she should have asked more questions of her father.

Still, he hadn't really given her much opportunity. He had passed her off to James to get details like location, date and time. She remembered her father had sounded frail in a way that had made her uneasy—and eager to please.

She might not like this job, but she was not letting her father down!

And she was not letting that arrogant ass—who happened to be her boss—win!

"And I am certainly not being defeated by a coffee-pot," she decided, and leapt to her feet. She focused furiously on her task, ignoring the almost constant jangling of the phone. The pot was a huge silver monstrosity that did not bear any resemblance to the one she had at home on her kitchen counter. She found grounds, dumped in approximately enough to sink the *Titanic,* found the on switch and got it working.

"'I like it strong.'" She mimicked his deep voice.

Still, when the office began to fill with the smell of coffee, Jessica King felt inordinately pleased with herself.

"There's no problem so great a good mind can't solve it," she said to herself, quoting Mitch. With new confidence she picked up the ringing telephone.

Okay, she might be in the shadow of her gorgeous younger sister, Chelsea, who the world and the press could not get enough of. And she was definitely in the shadow of Brandy, who was so bold and adventuresome.

But Jessie had her talents. She was the brainy princess, and K & B Auto—and Garner Blake—were about to find that out! That good-looking oaf didn't think she could do it. She couldn't think of a pleasure greater than proving him wrong.

"So, uh, Garner, what do you think?"

He didn't have to ask, "About what?" Clive, the best mechanic in his shop, looked like a biker and was as mild and shy as a groundhog fresh out of its hole. He and his wife had just had their first baby. Garner had been named godfather.

"She makes lousy coffee," he said, couching his answer in carefully diplomatic terms. What he was thinking was *I hate rich girls.*

In just a few moments of acquaintance she had called him mucky and tacky. The business he had spent his whole life building had been reduced to a mess and a mistake. She hadn't even known she was being insulting. She'd just been exercising that unconscious superiority of the very rich.

"I like the coffee," Clive said with just a touch of stubbornness. "Garner, you try being nice for a change, or she'll up and quit like all the rest of them."

We can only hope. Garner had chosen not to mention to these guys that their new office manager was one of *those* Kings. It would bring up a whole lot of questions that he didn't know how to answer.

"I ain't working here another week if you keep on trying to do all the jobs, including billing, booking and answering the phone."

Garner tried not to groan. Clive was going to make his stand over *this* girl, the one he *needed* to get rid of?

Resentfully, he reminded himself that his loyalty to this man who was threatening to quit was part of the reason he found himself in this predicament in the first place.

"Look, I'll run the business, you pull the wrenches."

"I miss your aunt," Clive said glumly.

Garner's aunt Mattie had done the office managing since he was a child. She was old and efficient and not the least distracting. Imagine her abandoning K & B for the dubious pleasure of marrying Arnold Hefflinger and moving to Quartzsite, Arizona! She'd given fair notice, but somehow Garner hadn't taken her seriously, or understood exactly how much she did and how hard she was going to be to replace, until it was too late.

"Them last two gals left in tears," Clive said, faint warning in the look he sent Garner.

But Garner could only hope it had been good practice for getting rid of this one. Though even as he thought it, he knew he didn't ever want to see Jessica King's big green eyes filming with tears.

Spitting with anger was another thing altogether.

"The second one looked awful good in a miniskirt," Clive remembered wistfully.

Garner sighed. Something they weren't going to have to worry about with Jessica King. She wasn't the miniskirt kind. In fact she looked like she had taken a wrong turn on the way to finding her kindergarten class—not what he'd expected at all. But those rich kids could be real good at that—the wolf-in-sheep's-clothing game.

Still, he'd expected, as a King princess, she would have been a whole lot flashier. Manicure, makeup, clothes, hair, jewelry. Jessica's hair had been a pretty color, but short, flattened to her head in a very unflattering manner. The boxy, refrigeratorlike design of the suit had successfully disguised any lines beneath it, which was a good thing. Her nails had been neat and filed. The only jewelry had been *that* ring.

She had the attitude, though, in spades. Mucky, tacky and messy, he reminded himself.

"I hope she brings cookies to work," Clive said.

"That girl hasn't ever baked a cookie in her life," Garner said.

"What would make you say that?" Clive asked innocently.

Garner stifled a snort. One thing he knew for sure: Rich girls did not bake cookies.

But Clive saved him from having to reply by shuffling off to his bay, where Mrs. Fannie Klippenhopper's thirty-year-old Impala was up on the hoist.

Aunt Mattie, of course, had provided cookies. Cookies and comfort. She had been part den mother and part drill sergeant and the sad fact of the matter was she was going to be irreplaceable as the office manager of K & B Auto.

He was willing to bet Jake King's daughter not only hadn't ever baked a cookie, she hadn't ever canned peaches, ridden a public bus or worried over a bill, either. Despite her rather surprising academic achievement, normal—like working the front end of a garage—would not be in her life experience. Normal to her was probably denting a very expensive car and walking away from it with a shrug and an *oh well*.

Unwillingly, the look on her face when he'd zipped up his coveralls in front of her came to mind.

If he didn't know better he would have called it *hunger*.

She had poked a rather delectable tongue out between lips that he'd already been misguided enough to touch. Those lips had been plump and sensuous, and that had been before she licked them.

"Sheesh," he said to himself.

From the size of that rock on her finger, she was very engaged.

Dumb was bad for an office manager, but complicated was way, way worse.

And complicated was his mind insisting on asking questions that were none of his business. Like why did a girl wearing a ring like that look so, well, not in love? None of that telltale glow and way too interested in a man who was not her fiancé zipping up his pants. Plus chocolate before nine in the morning? That woman was not happy.

Rich women were never happy.

His mother had been the first to teach him that lesson, but he'd insisted on repeating it several times, most recently with Kathy-Anne Rice-Chapman.

Besides, the plain fact of the matter was, even without the complication of Jessica being Jake King's daughter, Garner did not consider himself good at reading the intricacies of the female of his species, with the possible exception of Aunt Mattie. Though he'd even misread his good aunt. He'd thought she was staying forever, pure and simple. Though his daddy had warned him, a long, long time ago there was no such thing as a woman who stayed forever, and Garner's mother had been a case in point.

Jessica King had been here only moments, and Garner realized he was contemplating the most miserable moments of his life. It was not a good omen.

Garner Blake was good with cars. He read cars the way scholars read books. He could rebuild an old one until it purred like a kitten. He could ferret out the most elusive of mechanical problems. When parts didn't exist he could manufacture them. There was a science of sorts to cars. As far as he could tell, women did not come with the same predictable set of rules as the mechanical workings underneath the hood.

He had spent two days getting out every old box of files and bills he could find to scare Jessica King right off his place. Now he had upped the ante by daring her to last more than two hours. Of course, hearing the mousetrap go off under her desk had made him up his bet.

"Rich girls do not like rodents," Garner said cheerfully. He consulted his watch. One hour and fifty-one more minutes to go.

Garner sank down at his desk, took a sip of coffee and winced. As ungrateful as Clive would be for it, he felt responsible for Clive's child, or at least for the livelihood of that child's father. He had not missed the veiled threat in Jake King's voice during that last phone call. But if she left on her own, gave up, tossed in the towel…

He sighed. He had his own lawyers researching documents now, but it didn't look promising.

"You want *what?*" his lawyer had said. "Garner, those documents were likely signed two or three decades ago. I don't think this firm handled it."

So why was Jake King digging up decades-old dirt? Garner had known, of course, that Jake owned half the building. Years ago, as soon as he'd cleared up the wreckage of his father's mismanagement, he'd offered to buy Jake out. The offer had been rejected without explanation. Now this. Did Jake really have a say-so in how Garner ran his business? Did Jake own more than half the building?

Thinking of the legal tangle that could cause made Garner's head hurt.

What was that old devil, Jake King, up to?

And why on earth would he send his daughter here, straight into the camp of the enemy?

Maybe he doesn't like her, Garner mused, but Jessica King did not have the look—or the attitude—of a child not liked. He suspected she had been adored.

With relief, he remembered he had to look at her damaged car. If she was only going to be here another hour and forty-nine minutes, there needed to be no hitches to her leaving. He abandoned the coffee happily and began to whistle the moment he got behind the wheel.

Chapter Two

Jessie glanced at the clock and tried not to moan out loud. It was only ten-thirty. She was exhausted. So far she had made more coffee than Starbucks on a busy morning, and despite the fact she knew darn well it was not particularly good coffee, it kept disappearing.

She had driven two clients, who were leaving their vehicles at K & B for the day, back to their homes. It had given her an intriguing look at a lovely small town, which she might have enjoyed more if the shop truck, a big and finicky Dodge Diesel, didn't stall on a hair. Upon delivery to his home, one of the customers had glared at her, slammed the door and limped away holding his neck. Rattled from that, she had gotten lost on a back road of Farewell.

She'd finally returned to find a description of her job on her desk. As she was frowning over that page-long list of duties, a mechanic, Pete, had come in and wanted a part ordered. Another, Clive, arrived with a work order for a brake job for which she was supposed to figure out the charge. Clive had helpfully showed her an ugly and nearly indecipherable book called the labor book.

She had not made any headway on the mess, on a pile marked "urgent" apparently by one of her predecessors or on any of the leaning stacks of paper. The phone rang without letting up. To complicate matters more, every time the door opened from the work area, some traitorous part of her clenched in anticipation. It might be *him*.

Jessie considered her mind exceedingly disciplined, but this morning it was playing the traitor. It was conjuring visions of Garner Blake's dark, sardonic eyes, the line of his lip, the broadness of his shoulder. It was hard enough learning a new job without the distraction of a man like that. And even allowing herself to think of him made her feel guilty, as if she was being unfaithful to lovely, sweet, *intelligent* Mitch.

So she invented a little game. When Garner Blake's rather formidable male form crowded into her mind, she would call it a name.

"Insensitive boor."

"Neanderthal."

"Self-centered lunkhead."

"Poster boy for Mechanics R Us."

Of course, she really didn't know very much about him, but men like that were so easy to read. Self-assured, self-centered, self, self, self, selfish.

As entertaining as her little game was, the sheer amount of chaos she was trying to dig out from under was making her feel overwhelmed and utterly defeated.

She was in way over her head and even felt disturbingly close to tears.

On the other hand, when she snuck another look at the clock she realized she had only twenty-three minutes to go before she'd won the bet! Though the heat made it unlikely, she was beginning to hope Garner Blake wore long johns, not boxers. After she'd seen him keep his part of the bargain, she could phone her father and tell him she wasn't staying.

She had just stripped off her suit jacket, found the Impala in the labor book and figured out how many hours a brake job was slated to take, when the outer door to the shop swung open.

An elderly gentleman, looking very dapper in his hat and matching sports jacket, came in. He had a dog on a leash. He smiled shyly at her, helped himself to coffee and pulled a stool up to the counter. "I'm Ernie," he said after a moment, "and this is my dog, Bert. I did that on purpose. Ernie and Bert."

"Nice to meet you." She wasn't quite sure that it was. He had let go of Bert's leash and the dog was on her side of the counter, pressing his wet snout under her skirt.

"Er, can I help you with something?" She tried to push the dog away.

"Yes. Is there any cream?" Ernie asked shyly, apparently unaware his dog was being exceedingly rude.

Was there any cream? Was it part of her job to fetch cream in an auto shop? It wasn't a café, after all. A fridge, nearly lost among the other debris, gurgled helpfully. Sure enough there was cream in it. The dog, which looked like a basset crossed with a poodle, trailed her every step.

When she brought the cream that was all the encouragement Ernie needed. He began to talk, and he didn't stop. When he was partway through his eighth birthday party celebrated in the Great Depression, the dog pressed his nose right up her skirt and moaned plaintively. She looked at her watch, excused herself and fled into the back.

"Where's Mr. Blake?"

Clive lifted his head and looked at her, astonished. "Mr. Blake? Oh, you mean Garner?"

She nodded.

"Through there. Problem?"

Yes, there was a problem. She was done. She could not be a taxi driver, switchboard operator, brake biller, coffee-shop waitress, professional listener. She was not going to have rude dogs sniffing her skirt and moaning. It was too much to expect of one person.

Besides, things had been left undone for too long in this office. The work was mountainous. There wasn't enough instruction. How could she do any work with that man babbling away out there? The phone ringing? The dog…well, never mind the dog.

To add to that, there was no air-conditioning, and she was sweating through her lovely silk shell.

She burst into the bay where Garner was bent over her damaged Cadillac.

It looked different than the other bays. Spotlessly clean, for one.

He came out from under the hood, regarded her mildly, his gaze lingering just a little too long on where the sweat pooled between her breasts and made her silk top stick to her. Then he looked at his watch. He had the audacity to smile.

"Yes?" he said hopefully.

It was the hopefulness that made her forget the mountains of work, the interruptions, the extra duties, the dog and the sweat.

"There is a man out there I don't quite know what to do with," she said.

Disappointment crossed his features. "Oh, 10:31. Ernie, right?"

"And Bert!"

"I keep some cookies just under the counter. Give one to Bert."

That's why the stupid dog had been accosting her. He wanted his cookie.

He ducked back under the hood, dismissing her. "Oh, and Ernie likes cream in his coffee. It's in the fridge."

"Are you running a coffee shop or a garage?" she asked, aware of the snip in her voice.

"Some days I guess it's a little of both," he said.

"He wants my undivided attention," she said and heard the frustrated wail in her voice. "I need to figure out a bill for Clive and order a part for Pete, and the phone doesn't stop ringing. I don't have time to listen to him!"

"He's lonely." Garner came back out from under the hood, wiped his hands on a towel, regarded her cynically, his eyes branding her as superficial.

"Can't he go be lonely somewhere else?" Jessie said, and was appalled at how callous she sounded. "I'm not much of a multitasker," she added defensively.

His lips twitched suspiciously and even though Garner's expression didn't change, she could hear the smug smile in his voice. "Then, lady, you took a wrong turn at Main Street. This isn't the place for you."

"I've made it two hours," she said.

"Not quite." He ducked back under the hood.

"I think we can call it two hours. We're only ten minutes short of it."

"Nope. I have to consider what's at stake. Are you leaving the minute those two hours are up?"

She contemplated that. Certainly when she'd marched in here that had been her intention. No one could blame her, not even her father. Now she wasn't so sure she would give the insensitive, self-centered boorish Neanderthal the satisfaction.

"I'm not leaving," she shocked herself by saying. "I just need to know the official office policy on Ernie."

"Okay. Official—Give the dog a cookie. Give Ernie some cream for his coffee. Listen to a story or two, if that's not too big a chore for a princess."

She felt the insult of it. Had he been under the hood of this car conjuring up names for her in the same fashion she'd been doing to him? But that would mean he'd been thinking about her, and men like him simply didn't think about girls like her.

Did they?

"That hardly seems professional," she said after a moment.

He came back up, looked at her long and steady. He did not, she decided, look anything like a Neanderthal, those features so cleanly cut. But that didn't mean he wasn't one in his every attitude. Princess, indeed.

"You have to figure out what's important and what isn't," he said quietly.

It felt, ridiculously, like the Neanderthal was giving *her* instructions for her life. What was important in her life? And what wasn't? And why was it that in six years of obtaining a higher education, she had never asked herself that? Two hours on the front line, and it felt like everything, including her hard-won self-confidence, was disintegrating.

"Have you ever heard this Vietnamese proverb?" Garner asked, and his eyes were locked on hers, deep, dark and challenging. "When you eat fruit, think of the person who planted the tree."

She stared at him, nonplussed. That was the last thing she had expected to come out of his mouth. Poetry, for God's sake. Philosophy. Foreign philosophy at that!

He was supposed to be hiding a Neanderthal under that glorious exterior. What if he wasn't?

She felt, and hid, a little ripple of shock. Garner Blake was not what she thought a typical mechanic was. He was not what she needed him to be if she was going to tame this horrible guilt-inducing *awareness* of him.

"I may not have a master's degree," Garner said, "or a trillion-dollar trust fund, but I know that man, who has lived through a depression and served in a war. He's the one who planted the tree you and I are enjoying the fruit from today."

Her mouth fell open.

"In a business like this," he said, "caring about people has to be part of it. They can go get their cars fixed way cheaper in a bigger place. And you can't pretend you care about them, either. It has to be the real deal."

She hated that. That this big brooding ignoramus in front of her seemed to think he knew more about what was important than she did. And that he was so obviously the real deal.

What did that make her?

"You know what's important?" she snapped at him.

He raised a dark eyebrow.

"I made it two hours!"

He nodded, glanced again at his watch. "Jumping the gun again. According to my watch you have six minutes left."

She marched out of there. Ernie was still nursing his coffee, the dog gave her a betrayed look, which she fixed by finding the jar of enormous dog cookies behind the counter.

Six minutes left. She took the stool beside Ernie. "Okay," she said. "You were talking about the Depression. Your birthday, I believe."

He stared at her, stunned. A light went on in his faded eyes, and his hand covered hers. "Thank you for listening to me."

She felt ashamed of her own impatience. He was probably the same age as her father. How was it her father seemed so much younger and more vital? So driven and purposeful?

The door to the back bays opened and the two mechanics, Clive and Peter, came out. Garner followed a few minutes later.

She didn't miss his glance at the clock. She tamed an impulse to stick out her tongue at him. She watched as he strode across the office, bent over and rummaged under her desk. He came back across the room and tossed something down in front of her.

She met the challenging look in his eyes, before looking down.

There was a mouse in a trap.

"The building's old," he said with fake apology. "No matter what we do, we can't seem to get rid of the mice. Infested."

She knew exactly what he wanted, and she was inordinately pleased that she was not going to be giving it to him.

Garner Blake glanced at the clock. One minute to go. She was going to take one look at that mouse and probably faint dead away.

Hysterics would be fun.

Ah, yes, the little princess meets real life in rural America. And runs from it. Hopefully, at top speed.

He moved a little closer to her so he could grab her if she went pale and started to slide from her chair. He hoped he wouldn't have to. She'd removed her jacket, and the top she was wearing molded curves delectable enough to make a man's mouth go dry—without any kind of touching.

Oh, yeah, it was perfect. She had the deer-in-the-headlights look as she gazed at his offering.

Then she lifted her eyes to his.

They were green and clear, and there wasn't even a trace of hysteria in them.

"That isn't a mouse," she said, "it's a vole. See how sharp its nose is?"

She picked up the trap and held it toward him. Garner, before he could catch himself, took a hasty step away. A grin split her face and it changed everything about her. In an instant she went from being far too sober, too refined, too rich, to looking like a girl who was brimming with mischief and life.

He felt a ripple of shock.

It was now very apparent to him that Jessica King was not even close to being what he thought she was.

That was too bad. Because what he had thought was not the least appealing.

And this girl in front of him, inspecting the dead mouse—vole—with grave interest was appealing in a way he didn't even want to think about.

The guys all laughed at her reaction, knowing damn well he'd hoped for quite a different one. Clive gave him a very unsubtle *be nice* look.

"It's not even a deer mouse," she said with a touch of disdain. "I might have been afraid of that. Hanta virus carrier."

What the hell was she studying at university? Obviously not what he had thought: Mansion Decorating 101 and Social Climbing 303.

After that, it was guy talk over morning coffee. Cars. Baseball. Fishing. The princess, unfortunately, didn't look the least bit bored. In fact, she rather looked as though she was enjoying rubbing shoulders with the common folk.

And the mischievous light burning in her eye deepened when there was finally a break in the conversation. "Garner and I had a small bet this morning."

She had their full attention, and she enjoyed every minute of it.

"He seemed to think I was the wrong person for this job."

"Hey, two hours doesn't make you employee of the year!" he said.

"The bet wasn't whether I was going to be employee of the year. The bet was whether I would make it two hours or not. And gentlemen, I have!"

There was hooting and loud applause. He saw the pleasure flash across her face at the rowdy male approval, and he realized that probably sealed it. Miss Jessica King wasn't going anywhere.

"What was the bet?"

"Clive, I'm so glad you asked," she said sweetly. "The bet was if I made it working here for two hours, Garner was going to eat his shorts."

This announcement was followed by great guffaws and knee-slapping.

"I'll bring you some Tabasco, boss," Clive said. "That will help them go down a bit easier."

"Just a hint from me," Ernie said. "I'd launder them first."

This sent everyone, except Garner, into fits of laughter. Though he had to admit there was a little bubble of laughter inside of him. For the first time in a long time.

When had he last felt happy?

Before Kathy-Anne, he realized. His rich girl.

He looked at his watch. "Coffee break is over." He turned to her, "And two hours isn't a whole day, Miss MBA."

"Would you care to make another bet?" she asked sweetly.

"Dog cookies!" Clive howled. "Bet him a bowlful of dog cookies."

"No more bets," Garner said firmly.

He realized that meant something. He thought she was staying. And from the look in her eyes, almost surprised, she thought she was, too.

Sarah Jane MacKenzie flipped through channels, then shut off the TV with an irritated snap, got up and paced the confines of her tiny garage-top apartment.

"Thirty channels," she complained, "and nothing to watch."

She was aware of the irony of her boredom. Only a month ago living in a place like this with thirty channels to surf through would have been enough to make her feel as if she had died and gone to heaven.

The apartment over Jake King's six-bay garage was on

the Kingsway estate, and it was just a stone's throw from the main house. The space was like something out of a dream for a girl who had come from leaking roofs, peeling paint, mice infestation and mismatched, broken furniture.

Her apartment consisted of a small living room divided from a tiny kitchen by an eating counter. There was one bedroom, and a bathroom with a full-size tub. Every stick of furniture, dish, appliance and surface sparkled with cleanliness.

The colors of the walls and draperies were bold—rich honey-mustard-yellow meeting forest-green. The floors were ceramic tile, and the ceilings had fascinating angles. All in all, the space was like a dream student apartment featured in a decorating magazine, small and uncluttered, but practical and cozy.

And Sarah's life had become like something out of a storybook.

She worked for Jake King. She was making what she considered to be a phenomenal salary—twelve dollars an hour. She had been given a place to live. Chelsea King had personally provided her a wardrobe full of designer labels. One pair of those Chelsea cast-off jeans would have cost Sarah a week's salary! She harbored the hope that maybe she and Chelsea were becoming friends. But of course, here alone tonight, bored and restless, that felt just plain dumb.

As soon as her sister's wedding was over, Chelsea had departed for the condo she owned in California, saying she was in dire need of Los Angeles–style shopping. Sarah had thought a shopping trip probably meant a day or two, but two weeks had gone by and there had been no word from Chelsea.

If they were really friends, Chelsea would have called.

"We aren't friends," Sarah said crankily. "You're the charity case, she's the rich girl."

But Sarah was too aware of the injustice. She should be a rich girl, too. She was Jake King's granddaughter and the granddaughter of Fiona MacKenzie. Her own mother, Jake and Fiona's love child, had been a half sister to Brandy, Jessie and Chelsea. But Sarah was the only one who knew.

"Tell him," she told herself. She wanted to. She didn't want to. When she had brought baby Becky to him, Sarah had called him Grandpa Jake, supposedly for the baby, but trying it out for herself, too. The name had tasted both beautiful and bitter on her tongue.

Tell him? She'd had perfect opportunities. Was there a small worm of doubt in her that she really was his granddaughter, even if the secret diary she had found of her grandmother's said it was so? Even though she looked much like Jake and almost like Brandy's twin?

Why hadn't she said anything yet? She felt oddly protective of him. It was obvious his health was failing. What if the truth upset him? And what if the response to her secret was not one of joy and welcome?

There was a risk that she could lose the few crumbs she was being thrown. And she had come to love her little apartment and the wonderful clothes. How could she go back to what she had been before? A nobody waitress in Hollow Gap, Virginia, sweating how to pay her bills and shopping at the Goodwill store?

The problem, Sarah decided, was that the wedding was over. Everyone in this whole huge household, staff and family, had been rushing around in a fever pitch getting ready for Brandy and Clint's big day. She had been a part of something large and wonderful. Everyone had felt like family.

Then there had been Cameron.

Sarah's heart did a flip-flop in her chest and her stomach knotted.

Clint McPherson's younger brother had been amazing. Handsome. Fun-loving. Intelligent. Successful.

She could have sworn he was attracted to her. She could have sworn he might call.

"Yeah," she said cynically. "As if he'd call the likes of you. And do what, Sarah Jane? Fly in for a date? All the way from California? That's not your world."

But wasn't that the whole problem? What was her world? Where did she belong?

For a few weeks, it had seemed like she was a real member of a different kind of family, the kind you saw on TV and on the front of Christmas cards. But now everything seemed empty and dull, and she felt crushed. She was not Chelsea's real friend. Cameron McPherson was never going to call her.

She was a pretender.

It was easier to be a waitress trying to figure out how to get the heat turned back on in her dumpy rented house than to be filled with these larger-than-life dreams.

Sarah had never felt quite so lonely as she did tonight. She had never had time for loneliness before. Her every waking moment had been filled with worry.

She glanced at the clock. It was nearly midnight. She looked out her window and could see the office in the big house across the way.

Was the house locked? Maybe if she went and worked for a few hours…

Happy to have a plan—any plan—Sarah skipped

down the narrow steps of her apartment and across the paved car yard. The front door wouldn't be open, obviously, the whole house was probably alarmed. She was just about to turn away when she saw a light go on in the kitchen. She went and tapped lightly on the back door.

One of the kitchen staff opened it cautiously. Sarah was aware of the way the girl's face closed when she saw her.

The house staff didn't like her. They hadn't liked her from the beginning, and they liked her even less now that she had been befriended by Chelsea and had actually been a *guest* at Brandy and Clint's wedding, not a member of the staff.

"I can't sleep," she said. "I thought I might go to work for a while."

The girl hesitated, but word of Chelsea's upbraiding of the girl who had told Sarah her clothes looked like they had come from a thrift store had obviously gotten around, because she stepped back reluctantly from the door.

Sarah saw she was preparing a tray. "Is that for Mr. King? I could take it to him."

Her grandfather was a good man, kind, so accepting of her. Suddenly she longed to talk to him. Maybe tonight she would tell him the whole truth, that she was the granddaughter of Fiona, the woman he had loved a long, long time ago. That she was his family as surely as his beloved daughters, his granddaughter as surely as Becky was now his granddaughter.

But the kitchen assistant recoiled from her offer to bring the tray to Jake, and Sarah saw hostility in her eyes.

"I'm to take the tray to Mr. King," she said tightly, as if Sarah was trying to usurp her position.

"All right," Sarah said, holding her hands up in mock surrender and scooting by her. The house was creepy at night. Dark shadows played off pieces of furniture that probably had been around for hundreds of years. There were probably ghosts in here!

She practically ran to the familiar sanctuary of the office, flung open the door and turned on all the lights. She felt safe. She went to her desk and picked up the photos she had been working with that day.

This was her job—to chronicle the privileged lives of the women, who though her age, were her aunts. A photo album for each of them. Sarah had painstakingly sorted the pictures into time periods, and she was currently working on Jessie's teen years.

Soon she was immersed in it. She thought, despite her friendship with Chelsea—her sort of friendship with Chelsea—that maybe she liked Jessie the best of her aunties. Jessie seemed more vulnerable than her outgoing sisters. In many of the pictures, she was slightly apart, as if she did not belong to this world of wealth and privilege or as if she did not want to. She was not quite as perfect as her outgoing sister, Brandy, or her gorgeous sister, Chelsea. She had battled with plumpness during her teen years. And had braces and glasses. Many of the photos were of her sitting under a tree with a book—

"Hmm, hmm."

Sarah gave a little shriek. Mr. King's assistant, James, was standing at the door of the office.

He was in a light blue silk housecoat and slippers, and he looked so silly, so different from how he normally looked in his expensive suits, that Sarah giggled nervously.

It was a mistake. He didn't like her anyway, and now his mouth tightened.

"What are you doing?" he asked.

"I c-c-couldn't sleep," she said nervously. "I thought I'd come get some work done."

"I don't want you in here by yourself."

The words were spat out coldly.

She heard everything he wasn't saying. That she was trash. That she couldn't be trusted. That she wasn't good enough. That she didn't belong here and never would.

She got up from behind the desk. She was aware she was shaking, but with rage or frustration or just plain reaction, she wasn't quite sure.

Didn't she already know that she wasn't good enough to be a real member of this family even if a few drops of Jake's blood did flow through her veins? Didn't she already know that it was too late for her to learn how to use the right fork and wear the right clothes and do and say things befitting of one of the King princesses? Didn't she already know that she didn't deserve all the good things that had happened to her? That she was here on borrowed time?

When James saw her coming, he turned on his heel and walked out the door ahead of her, his weak chin set at a haughty angle.

So, he didn't trust her alone in Jake's office?

Without even missing a step, she palmed a very expensive-looking pen off Jake's desk as she moved by it. It was hidden inside the sleeve of her blouse when she brushed by James who turned to close the door behind her.

"Good night," he said, his voice stiff with judgment and dislike.

"Good night," Sarah said. Her heart was hammering in her throat, but she felt deliciously invigorated. Alive.

She went back to her apartment and opened a drawer. In it was a silver dish she had taken from Jake's office in the first few days she had worked for him. Since Chelsea had befriended her, and she had been invited to the wedding, that silver dish had filled her with guilt.

But tonight she didn't feel guilty about it at all. She put the pen in the drawer beside it and slammed it shut. These might be the only treasures she ever claimed from her grandfather, and she felt entitled to them.

Chapter Three

"This is way too much money to pay for a simple repair."

Jessica let her eyes slide to the clock. Nearly five o'clock. She was not sure she had ever had a longer day in her life. And that was before the arrival of Mrs. Fannie Klippenhopper in her flamboyant housedress and corkscrew pink curls. She was here to pick up her aging Impala.

"I can check the price again, Mrs. Klippenhopper. Maybe I got it wrong. It *is* my first day here." On the job description that Garner had left on her desk earlier, the very last line actually said learning all aspects of her position could take up to a year. With constant supervision.

Garner's constant supervision? She could feel her heart thudding. What would a year around a man like that—with his constant supervision, no less—do to a woman like her?

If Mrs. Klippenhopper was feeling any sympathy for first-day employees, it flagged instantly when she noticed Jessica's fast-fading attention. She cleared her throat. Jessica noticed her eyebrows were painted into a thin, permanent frown.

"The price is wrong," Mrs. Klippenhopper snapped. "It's not what I was quoted and I won't pay it."

"I can't find the quote," Jessica explained again. "If you would just tell me what the quote was, or the general vicinity of it, we could—"

"You stupid cow, I told you I can't remember!"

Jessica flinched as if she'd been struck. Stupid cow?

Six years in university, to be called stupid while working at the front counter of an auto-repair shop? Tempting as it was to fit in a less-than-casual mention of her education, or the fact that it was supposed to take a year to learn this job, Jessica doubted those details would alter the pinched, ready-for-war look on Mrs. Klippenhopper's face one little bit.

Had she really called her a cow? Her insecurities were riding close to the surface after her first day in this foreign environment. Jessie immediately concluded the suit *did* make her look fat. The silk top had melted in the heat and was now molding every extra ounce of her.

She looked longingly past Mrs. Klippenhopper's shoulder at the door that led to the street. It would be so easy to gather her purse and walk right out, leaving this horrible woman standing there, stewing.

She could feel tears smarting behind her eyes. Not sad tears, but emotion brought on by suppressed fury and exhaustion and pure frustration. It occurred to her that even as she had distanced herself from the role of a King princess, she had always accepted—and expected—the perks that came with it.

Such as being treated with respect. Is this what her father had meant by a taste of the real world? Did people treat each other like this? Had she ever treated anyone in a service position badly?

Certainly she had never called anyone a stupid cow, but she could remember being impatient. Intolerant.

"I could have you fired," Fannie said, and there was no mistaking the satisfaction in her voice as she contemplated the delicious power of her position.

That was it! The last straw. She simply didn't have to take this kind of treatment. Jessica King was done being polite. "You know what? There is nothing I would like more than—"

To be fired. Then she wouldn't have to quit. But before she could get the words out, and several more along with them, the connecting door to the service bays whispered open.

Out of the corner of her eye, she saw him.

How ridiculous to think of him as any kind of savior!

She had not seen him since coffee break this morning, and somehow she had forgotten in that short span of time what a commanding presence he had.

Garner had taken off the coveralls and was in the jeans and T-shirt she had first seen him in this morning. It seemed so unfair. She had wilted like a petunia in full sunlight, and he was looking crisp and fresh and as if he didn't feel the heat at all.

Except, was that a tiny bead of sweat going down his neck? And if it was, why was it heart-stoppingly sexy on him and just plain ugly on her?

Jessica noted, reluctantly, that despite the plainness

of his garb, there was no denying Garner Blake carried himself with an innate sense of who he was. He moved like a prince, like royalty, and she could see the irony of that. All her life she had been labeled one of America's princesses, but she didn't carry the essence of that within her. If she did, Fannie wouldn't dare treat her like this! Stupid cow, indeed!

But Garner Blake, proprietor of a grubby little auto-repair business in nowhere, Virginia, exuded an aura, a confidence, a certainty, that would have put most real royals to shame.

"There," Jessie said brightly, trying to keep the wobble out of her voice, "just the man you were looking for."

Garner took in the situation, glanced at Fannie, then focused with unsettling intensity on Jessica. His eyes narrowed. She suspected he was a man who missed nothing, and he had not missed either the wobble in her voice or the suspicious brightness in her eyes.

One push from him, and she would be over the edge. If he took Fannie's side, or humiliated her in front of this awful woman, she felt like she would be done. Not just the job, but it felt as if something in her would break, something that could not be fixed.

She hated it that he seemed to sense how totally vulnerable she felt, so she masked every feeling she had and jutted out her chin, folded her arms over her chest, tapped her toe as if all she felt was impatience to have this situation dealt with so she could get out of here.

He didn't fall for any of it. He looked at her so searingly she felt her soul was exposed. And then the worst thing happened. The darkness in his eyes melted into something softer.

Sympathy!

The last thing she wanted from Garner Blake was sympathy. Still, how was it that he was constantly surprising her, making her feel off balance? She turned hastily to the desk, planning to pack the few meager things that had come out of her purse and get out of K & B Auto for good.

There, he'd won. He wanted to get rid of her anyway, and now his excuse was standing at the counter looking daggers at Jessica. But Mrs. Klippenhopper's sour expression transformed into one of soft delight as Garner turned his attention to her. Even her eyebrows managed to lift out of their evil *V.*

"Hello, Garner," she said sweetly.

"Mrs. Klippenhopper," he said. He glanced once more at Jessica. She plopped down at the desk and pretended to be furiously engrossed in some of the paperwork there. Again, he did not seem to be fooled. If she had more hair she would have used it to shield the side of her face from his scrutiny.

"Is there a problem?" he asked. The question was directed at her, not Fannie Klippenhopper. Jessica shrugged.

"Your new girl can't find the quote for my car, and she keeps giving me the wrong price, which is extraordinarily high." The woman lowered her voice confidentially, but Jessica still heard every word. "She's been very rude to me."

Jessica whirled in her chair. Who had been rude to whom? She could not believe the look of wounded innocence on Fannie's face.

"And me a senior citizen," Fannie reminded him.

If he was looking for an excuse to fire her, there it was!

She hoped he did. She wanted to be fired. She never wanted to deal with the likes of Mrs. Klippenhopper again.

But if he fired her, she knew a part of her would shrivel up and die.

Garner picked up the bill that was still lying on the counter and studied it for a moment. Jessie couldn't even pretend to be interested in what was on her desk.

His face was a study in serious contemplation, but unless she was mistaken, his lips were twitching. And not with annoyance, either. Garner was trying not to laugh!

If he found this funny, Jessica was not sure that she could be held responsible for her actions. Her hand closed around a stapler. If he laughed at her distress, she was throwing it at him.

It did not matter that she was not the kind of woman who threw staplers. She had experienced a stressful day. Funny how she thrived on stress at university—deadlines, projects, exams—she loved them all. But this was a totally different kind of stress. It changed people. She could clearly see that now.

She felt a moment's pity for people who lived lives where they faced challenges like this all the time, in the course of their duties. Maybe that was what her father had meant about the real world.

Had she lacked compassion for others in her life?

Easier to focus on Garner and the lack of compassion she felt about his obvious amusement over this situation than to face those tougher and larger questions about herself.

But Garner had tamed his smile so thoroughly that she wondered if she might have imagined it in the first place. He glanced at her one more time and he gave her a little wink. The wink changed everything. It put them

on the same team. In a flash, it made Mrs. Klippenhopper pathetic and amusing instead of powerfully and ig-
norantly mean-spirited.

He reached for an untidy-looking binder under the
counter and looked something up. He slid it back under
the counter.

He gave his full attention back to Mrs. Klippenhopper. "Let's not worry about the bill today. I'll send you
a bill when I find the quote."

"Oh, that would be lovely," Mrs. Klippenhopper said,
and sent Jessie a see-how-it's-done look. She marched
out the door and got in her car.

Garner pulled the big binder back out from under the
counter. "Come on over here."

It would be easier to just quit than go over there and
find out what she had done wrong. Still, she was drawn
to him as if pulled by an invisible string. She stood
beside him at the counter.

Her head barely came to his shoulder. It made her
feel small and delicate, and like the farthest thing in the
world from a stupid cow.

"This is the quote book," he said. He told her how it
worked. It was a very basic system, nothing the least
bit dangerous about it. Yet Jessie felt she was in the
danger zone.

Because his voice was gentle and patient, not the
voice of a man who concurred that she was a stupid cow.
And the scent coming off him was like a little bit of
heaven—aftershave and soap, the faintest whiff of
something she could have sworn was leather and something so intoxicating it had to be pure man.

"So—" he passed her the book "—see if you can find
the quote for Fannie Klippenhopper."

She did. She stared at it. She lifted her eyes to his. His were lit with good humor.

The price Fannie Klippenhopper had been quoted for the job on her Impala was actually twenty-three dollars higher than the price Jessie had given her.

"Why, that bossy old fool!" Jessie said. "She's still sitting out there. I'm going to tell her."

A hand on her arm stopped her. He shook his head. *Don't say it,* she ordered herself. But her voice disobeyed. "She called me a stupid cow!"

"Oh, yeah, she calls everybody that. My aunt used to put an extra twenty bucks on the bill for every time she got it."

"Oh." She brightened immeasurably. "It wasn't personal, then?"

"Personal? I don't get that. What do you mean personal? She's a difficult, old woman. How could that be about you?"

She scowled at him. She had been attacked. How could he possibly make that sound as if she thought the world revolved around her? Did she have to spell it out to him? "As in she thought I was stupid, personally. And a cow."

He studied her intently. "No one who talked to you for more than three seconds would sincerely think you were stupid. You have MBA written all over you."

"It's not exactly an MBA."

"Whatever. They're all MBAs to us dunces who run the mechanic shop."

"Anyone who talked to you for more than three seconds would know you aren't a dunce, Garner."

"You better stop," he said. "This is sounding suspiciously like a truce."

"What were we fighting about?"

He was looking at her as if he could drown in her eyes. She was not sure anyone had ever looked at her with quite that intensity before.

It made the bottom fall out of her stomach as if she was riding a high-velocity roller coaster.

"I don't remember," he said softly.

She shook herself free of the spell of his eyes. It took quite a bit of effort.

"And the cow part?" she asked tentatively.

"What about that part?"

"It wasn't personal?"

"In what way could that be personal?"

If she wasn't careful, she was going to fall in love. "You know…" Her voice trailed off.

"No, I don't."

She glared at him. Was he going to make her spell it out for him? He was! "Was she implying I'm just a teensy bit, um, overweight?"

A stupid question to ask a near complete stranger who was so devastatingly good-looking, the stars probably gazed at him at night.

A stupid question to ask a man whose eyes were so direct and so full of…well, something.

Sexiness, her inner voice supplied helpfully.

"You aren't fat," he said softly, his voice as unintentionally seductive as a Serendipity frozen hot chocolate on a hot summer afternoon.

"I'm not?"

"Where would you get that idea?"

The mirror?

"You have curves, Jessie. Gorgeous, womanly curves that make any man with an ounce of testosterone want to, um, touch you, hold you."

Her mouth fell open.

He looked suddenly uncomfortable, as if he had said a whole lot more than he wanted to. His tone changed, and she knew he was deliberately inserting lightness into it, changing the mood between them that was suddenly as charged as the air before an electrical storm.

"That should earn me a letter from the sexual appropriateness police tomorrow," he said.

But she wasn't quite as ready as he was to let it go. "*You* don't feel that way, do you?" she squeaked.

He hesitated just long enough that they both knew the answer. But he said, in a shocked tone, "Me? No, of course not. I'm your boss. It's against the law to find female employees attractive."

"You find me attractive?" That terrible squeak was still in her voice.

The answer flashed, white-hot, through his eyes. His gaze was searing her lips, and then the curve of her neck. It touched like a hot iron on her ears. Her soul was branded.

"Is it important how I feel?" he asked uneasily. "I would think all that matters is how he feels." He touched the ring on her finger and then his hand dropped away. "Whoever gave you this."

For a full minute she had trouble thinking who that was. For way too long it felt as if her old life was dissolving and a new one was beckoning.

What would that world be like? That world of Garner Blake's? What would it be like having that reckless grin soften just for you? To have those eyes grow darker when they beheld you?

He realized he hadn't answered her question.

"Well, I might find you attractive," he said, and now

his tone was completely teasing. "If it wasn't against the law. And if you weren't a King."

"A King?" she said. "What does that have to do with anything?"

"Feuding families. Like the Hatfields and McCoys."

"Are you kidding?"

"No. It dates back a lot of years. To my grandfather. I thought it was over and done with until your father called me last week."

"But why would he send me here?"

"I don't know. I thought I was going to be able to wheedle it out of you."

The information just added to Jessie's sense of her world being oddly topsy-turvy, spinning in a direction she had no control over. She would call her father tonight and demand some answers.

She snapped the quote book shut and left Garner's side hurriedly, before she did something really dumb and out of character.

Like kissing her boss.

She didn't even know the man! But she was a biologist, and she knew all about the pull of attraction, the power of it. At least she knew the science of it. She had never been caught in that vortex herself. Until now.

She began to arrange items neatly in the small cleared area on the desk.

Guilt swept her hard. She was not allowed to think thoughts like this. She had said yes to another man. What kind of person was she to say yes to one man and to be so tempted by another?

A woman like her mother, she thought sickly. Her mother whose secrets she had guarded. Her mother who had died in the arms of a man who was not Jessie's father, but who quite likely was the father of her younger sister....

She picked up her jacket off the chair, shoved her arms into it.

"I won't be back," she said. "I'm sorry. I shouldn't have come here. I don't know why I did. I'm terrible at this job. Ask anyone. Ask Mrs. Klippenhopper."

The words were pouring from her mouth like babble, and he looked down at her, those dark eyes liquid pools of calm and strength. He stopped the flood of words with a finger on her lips.

She was possessed by a spirit that wanted to nuzzle it! Thankfully, he removed the temptation almost instantly.

"You're doing fine. The price you came up with for Mrs. Klippenhopper was fine, Jessie."

"You knew the quote was higher. Why didn't you tell her? Never mind. I don't care if you didn't stick up for me."

That sounded ridiculously juvenile, so she rushed on.

"I don't think I can do this job," she said, again, only this time she was shocked to find humiliating tears spark in her eyes. "I can't deal with people like her. She was so unreasonable. What gives a person a right to be mean like that?"

"She didn't used to be as bad. She lost her only grandson in Iraq a little while ago. She sees a bigger world, things outside of Farewell, as being responsible for that."

She felt grudging forgiveness in her heart for Mrs. Klippenhopper. "That doesn't explain why she was nasty to your aunt."

"She just hated my aunt, pure and simple. Aunt Mattie aged well. Reason enough for spite in one who hasn't. This is a truth about people—if you are bitter, tragedy will make you more so. If you're not, tragedy may challenge you to be more than you were before."

Jessie was taken aback, once again, by the pure depth of the man. He had, as far as she knew, not an iota of so-called higher learning, and yet he seemed wise in ways it would be very easy to want to explore. She didn't like this one little bit, this roller coaster of emotion that this man—one she barely knew, she reminded herself sternly—was creating within her.

Still, it made it even more urgent to get away from him, this man who was harboring a disconcerting sensitivity under his rough tough exterior.

As if he read her mind, he said softly, "Besides, you don't want to quit now."

"I don't?"

He shook his head solemnly. "At coffee tomorrow, I'm going to make good on my bet with you."

"You're going to eat your shorts?" she asked cynically.

He nodded.

She laughed.

"That's better."

She felt a strange shiver at that—that he had wanted to make her laugh, had wanted to take that hurt away.

And then she realized there had been the subtlest of changes between them—he was challenging her to stay instead of leave.

She knew she couldn't accept that challenge.

She knew the electricity arcing in the air between them was not a force the pudgy pragmatic princess had any hope of controlling. She had taken biology, all those years ago, hoping there was a scientific way to explain the riddle that had been her mother. There was, but she had disdainfully concluded the pulls of biology could be ignored by more-evolved species. Now she was not so sure.

So she should run, obviously.

On the other hand, was he really going to eat his shorts? What did he have up his sleeve? And why had her father sent her here? There was a little more to it than getting a taste of the real world. Could she leave without finding out?

Could she leave without having really conquered anything about the job?

Oh, sure, she'd survived a day. But she had made no headway on the mess, and her understanding of how things worked was very limited. She didn't have a year to learn the position, but she considered herself smarter than the average…princess. Could she conquer this challenge in one summer?

What would it say about her character if she quit? That she really was just a frilly little princess who ran away at the first sign of an obstacle, a challenge? The real world? In larger circumstances—a tragedy, for instance—how would that translate? Would she be the kind of person who became bitter or who became better?

She set her purse back down, took a deep, steadying breath, ordered herself to be cool and professional.

"As a matter of fact, I've been jotting down questions all day."

He groaned.

"We can leave it until tomorrow if you have someone waiting for you."

She could have kicked herself. It was not subtle at all. Besides, why did she care if he had a girlfriend?

She had a boyfriend. She was taken, taken, taken.

She was taken, all right—she had taken one step further down a road where she had sworn not to go.

"Nope," he said. "No one waiting for me." He slid her a look. Had he seen through her question to what she was really asking?

Was he taken? Attached?

"My latest love is an old car I've got in the garage behind my house."

"What kind?"

Oh! The impression she wanted to give was that she didn't give two figs about him, his personal life or his cars.

"It's an old Ford Mustang. A '67."

Stop, she ordered herself. "What color?"

"Burgundy."

She sighed with unintentional bliss.

"You really like old cars?" he asked.

They did not need anything in common. It was bad enough that he was not turning out to be any of the things she had expected he would be. He was not an Neanderthal. Or a lunkhead. He was not stupid. Or insensitive.

Poster boy for Mechanics R Us was debatable.

Somehow she could see him leaning over a car, in a white T-shirt, smiling, selling posters by the million.

"They're okay," she said, then hurriedly she turned to her desk. All day she had been stacking things in a questions file, and she pulled herself back to being professional.

"Could we go over these things?"

Then they were sitting side by side at her desk, his voice deep and low and sure, his shoulder big and strong where it touched hers.

Finally they had made their way through the stack of items.

He got up and stretched, arms tucked behind his neck, chest thrust forward, shirt pulled up slightly to expose the leanness of his stomach, the absolute sexiness of his belly button.

She gulped and gathered up her things.

"Well, I'll see you tomorrow then," she said.

"Turn around."

He plucked something off her behind, held it up for her inspection, laughing.

It was a piece of electrical tape. And then she was laughing too, laughing at herself, and life and him. It felt so good to laugh like that.

Unfortunately, she felt that disloyalty to Mitch again. What was she doing laughing with another man, over something so small and foolish?

And where was the laughter in her relationship with Mitch?

"Wear jeans tomorrow," he said, and went out the door.

"I don't own a pair of jeans," she said, but he was already gone.

Garner Blake cursed himself for most of the short walk home.

She'd been on the verge of quitting! He'd seen the total vulnerability shimmering in her eyes right after her encounter with old Fannie.

A smarter man would have just given her a little shove over the edge.

A little fat? Why, yes, ma'am, you are.

That would have sent Jessica King packing before any damage was done in Garner Blake's life.

But she wasn't fat. And those eyes, turned luminescent from unshed tears, had made him tell her.

"Gorgeous, womanly curves," had been his exact words. "Curves that make any man with an ounce of testosterone want to, um, touch you, hold you." Thankfully, he'd managed to stop himself there. If his fool mouth would have kept yakking, the full truth would have come out. Between the mystery of those eyes and the lushness of those curves a man felt driven to know her.

"Kiss her senseless," he muttered to himself.

Jessica King was stunning. And she was staying.

To be honest, he was glad. He didn't want the game to be over before it began.

He wanted to know what old man King was up to.

Sure, but he also wanted to know about all the complications of those sea green eyes.

He cursed to himself.

Man, did he like playing with fire.

But it didn't feel like he was playing with fire.

It felt as if he'd been earth-bound and something in her eyes beckoned to him to see if he could fly and touch the sky.

"I don't like rich women," he reminded himself sternly.

Mary Johnston popped her head out from behind her lilac shrubs. "You don't like what, Garner?"

"Nothing." Gee, wouldn't he like that getting all over town, that he was walking down the streets mumbling to himself.

He got home, let himself in. The house, which had been his grandfather's, seemed way too big and way too quiet. He made a quick phone call. Emma, at the bakery, was flabbergasted by his request, but told him she had adored him since he was a boy and would do anything for him. Then she added, "For a hundred bucks."

A hundred bucks well spent, he thought. He hung up

the phone and wondered where Jessica King was staying tonight.

"That would fall in the none-of-your-business category," he warned himself sternly.

Then he found himself wondering what she would look like in blue jeans instead of that uptight suit.

That was none of his business either, but he was going to find out anyway.

He ate supper out of a can, worked on the Mustang for a while with a surprising lack of enthusiasm.

When he went to bed he was aware he couldn't wait until morning.

And that he hadn't felt that way for a long, long time.

Chapter Four

The following morning Jessica King regarded herself critically in the full-length mirror of her hotel room. She was wearing a hip-hugging pair of jeans, and a bright orange T-shirt that said I Fared Well In Farewell.

The message suited her. She *had* fared well in Farewell—she had lasted not just hours, but a whole day. She had honored her father's wishes. She had survived an encounter with Fannie Klippenhopper.

Best of all, Jessie had won the bet with Garner Blake and she was ridiculously eager to see how he planned to make good on it. And, bonus, she had been told she had curves. Gorgeous, womanly curves that made men think gorgeous sexy thoughts. About her.

That kind of evaluation changed things. Take the outfits she was wearing. It was like a makeover in reverse. Her Chanel suit was now in a heap in the corner of the room. Gorgeous curves deserved tight jeans.

Still, Jessie wondered if the jeans were a bit too much. They were made of some wonderful stretch fabric that was the ultimate in comfort. But they did hug like a glove.

Did they make her look like she was trying too hard to be sexy?

Laughable. Her, Jessica King, sexy. Looking sexy was Chelsea's department.

Though not according to her new boss, she reminded herself, and felt that nice little tingle in her belly.

She really hadn't had much choice in jean selection, anyway. The local mercantile had featured three different styles, take them or leave them. And she liked how the jeans and T-shirt made her look, younger and more carefree, not the mature look that she always tried for around Mitch. He was older than her, more established in the academic world. It was natural that she had tried to fit in. But had that made her stodgy and matronly before her time? If so, why had Mitch approved?

Not that she wanted to think about Mitch. They had argued on the phone last night.

He had told her, after she had given him a few details about her day, that she should come home. And she hadn't even gotten to the part about being called a stupid cow!

The job, he had pointed out, was far beneath her qualifications.

She already knew that, but hearing it from him, the point had sounded judgmental and snobby. She wanted to tell him the position was challenging in a different way. She wanted to point out that any job that took a year to learn wasn't exactly for dummies.

But before she had a chance to say either of those things, Mitch said, "It's not as if you need the money."

They had never really discussed her money, her

father's great fortune, her trust fund. She received a monthly allowance, though pride made her do her best to live within the means she earned, not always successfully. She had weaknesses for good linens, antiques and wonderful cars.

Still, she thought money didn't matter. Ideas mattered in his world. That had always been a large part of his appeal and that of the academic community. But had there been the slightest shift since he'd been a guest at Kingsway for Brandy's wedding? That she would even ponder such a thing of dear, sweet Mitch just added to Jessie's guilt.

Her call to her father had been intercepted by his secretary, James, who had told her her father was in bed. Her father in bed at eight o'clock in the evening? It seemed preposterous. And worrisome.

"Is everything okay?" she'd asked.

James had assured her everything was fine, but she was certain she had heard the slightest hesitation in his voice.

Her former world seemed oddly troubled, as if a storm cloud hovered over it. So, instead of contemplating that, she contemplated the delight of the moment and did another experimental twirl in front of the mirror.

"I didn't look this young when I *was* this young!" she informed her reflection.

She looked, if not slender, every bit as gloriously curvy as Garner had claimed she was. In jeans! Who knew that could happen with the right pair of jeans? Well, probably Chelsea. Not that Chelsea would ever think a $24.95 pair of jeans was the right pair!

Maybe it wasn't the jeans making her feel like this.

Once a woman had been given a message like the one Garner had given her and seen the heat in a man's eyes when he gave her that message, was she able to see things about herself that she had been blind to before?

As a last touch, Jessie wet her hair, ran her gel-coated hands through it and gave it a shake. Was she even the same person she had been yesterday at this time?

The answer was no, and she knew it was not entirely because of the wardrobe changes.

Picking up her new denim bag, she headed out the door. She would have liked room service for breakfast, but this hotel—the only one in Farewell—did not provide it.

She found a small diner and arrived at her office at precisely five minutes to seven.

The door was open, and there was a long white box on the counter. It looked like the type of wonderful container that held long-stemmed roses. She touched it fondly. Mitch was losing no time in making amends for their little tiff last night. There had been very few of them over the course of their relationship.

Uneasily she wondered if it was because they had started out as teacher and student. Maybe in some ways, their relationship had not evolved. Did he talk and she listen? Was he faintly condescending when she offered her opinions?

She hated this. That she was questioning a relationship that had always felt infinitely stable and that she had always felt so fortunate to be in. She hated it that she was entertaining doubts. On the other hand, if she was going to have doubts, wasn't now the time to have them? Before they actually set a date? Before they actually said "I do" and "Until death do us part"?

Until death was a long, long time, after all! Wasn't it the most normal thing in the world for a bride-to-be to get the jitters?

She touched the florist's box, and closed her eyes. Like a little girl who believed in fairy tales, Jessie decided that if the box held white roses from Mitch, she would know everything was as it was meant to be, that she was destined to marry him, that she had made the right decision when she had said yes.

Then she frowned. What if it held yellow roses? Or red ones?

"Hey, don't touch that!"

She jumped back from the box, whirled and looked at her boss.

Garner was effortlessly handsome this morning—brown eyes clear and sparkling, freshly shaven, his dark hair still damp from the shower, his jeans clinging in all the right places. He had on a blue T-shirt, that showed off the formidable swell of his biceps, the perfect cut of his chest and the flatness of his belly.

"I like your shirt," he said.

She liked his eyes. And his muscles. And the set of his lips. But she wasn't sure if it would be appropriate to tell him that. Then she realized his shirt also had the message I Fared Well In Farewell.

So, instead of telling him all the things she liked, she said, "Thanks. Yours, too. The Ralph Lauren collection?"

"Yeah. Only $300. A steal."

She liked that he played effortlessly into her slightly warped sense of humor. It was so unfair. She was determined not to like any more about him than she absolutely had to.

And then he looked at her approvingly. "Ralph

Lauren aside, that outfit is way better for the job you are doing." And then more softly, "Way better on you."

Just say thank you and shut up. But apparently that was asking too much of herself. "In what way?"

"Yesterday you looked like an old-maid librarian. You had *sssshhh* written all over you."

What about gloriously curvy? she wanted to remind him. That was so much nicer than what he was suggesting: uptight, controlling, rigid.

But he took the sting out of the statement almost immediately. "Now you look like a girl a guy could drink beer with on the tailgate of his truck."

"Oh," she said with deliberate chill, even though in her mind's eye she could see it, sitting on the tailgate, chatting, laughing, the stars coming out. "Is that the big date in Farewell?"

A chill crept into his own eyes. "Naturally, you'd be used to much better things. For a moment you just looked a different part."

Maybe that was the problem with looking different parts—or looking into this man's eyes, for that matter. You could forget who you were.

"I'm not sure if looking like a girl who drinks beer on the tailgate of a truck is a compliment," she said regally, but she was not sure she totally managed to keep the regret from her tone. She would never be sharing the tailgate of a truck with this man.

"Have you ever tried it?"

"Of course not!"

"Well, don't knock it until you've tried it, or to paraphrase Herbert Spencer, 'contempt prior to investigation can keep a man in everlasting ignorance.' Or a woman."

She wished he wouldn't keep doing that—breaking

the stereotype she wanted to hold of him. Life would be so much safer if he was the dumb mechanic and she was the frivolous rich girl. "Who's Herbert Spencer?" she asked.

"Who knows?" he said with a careless shrug. "It's something I read a long, long time ago. But I never forgot it."

He read! Dammit, another chink out of the cretin defense.

"Don't touch the box," he warned again, gesturing at the roses. "It's a surprise for coffee time. No peeking."

"You brought the box?" she asked, horrified that it was not a peace offering from Mitch.

"Who did you think?" he asked with a faint edge of sarcasm. "The tooth fairy?" And then with one final glare in her direction, he went out the adjoining door.

What did it mean if there were flowers in it, and they were from Garner instead of Mitch?

Then Jessie snorted at her own whimsy. "The pragmatic one," she reminded herself.

Besides, Garner did not get her flowers! If he had, he would have scooped them up and thrown them away as soon as she knocked tailgate sitting. Or thrown them at her!

What did it mean that she was hoping, however faintly, that Garner was going to come back in here zipping up his coveralls, as he had yesterday?

"It means you are an idiot," she grumbled to herself.

To her amazement the morning went marginally better than yesterday morning had. It had nothing to do with that white box on the counter, and if it did, it was only because everyone enjoyed a mystery, a surprise.

What would it mean if Garner had got her flowers?

He didn't get you flowers, she told herself sternly. A

man like that did not buy a girl like her flowers. He had probably never bought flowers in his life. He was a man who thought romantic was having a beer on the tailgate of a truck! He probably bought six-packs of oil as gifts for the fairer sex!

"Or a jar of pickles to eat on the tailgate," she thought aloud, unkindly.

The only way he would have bought flowers was if he wanted something. A light clicked on in her head—like not to eat his shorts.

That was it, she decided. He was trying to bribe his way out of fulfilling his side of the bet.

At ten-thirty, Ernie came in. She got Bert a dog cookie and fetched the cream from the fridge. She listened to his stories for a few minutes before the rest of the guys arrived for coffee.

And then Garner was at the counter, making a great ceremony of clearing his throat.

"As you all know," he said, "I made a bet yesterday that I lost."

This was greeted with hooping and hollering, which Jessie joined with far more enthusiasm than a well-educated woman, noted for her reserve, should have displayed.

"I promised if Jessie was still here two hours after she started, I'd eat my shorts. And that's just what I'm going to do. And you all are going to help me."

"I ain't helpin' you," Clive muttered.

With a flourish, Garner opened the white box.

It did not contain white roses, or yellow ones, or red ones. The box did not contain flowers of any sort.

Something even better was inside that long, narrow white box. It held a cake, shaped exactly like a pair of boxer shorts. The baker had done a wonderful job: the cake was iced in purple with pink polka dots.

In white icing was the bold message "Eat My Shorts."

He bowed to her. "You said you'd prefer boxers."

She found herself blushing. "I didn't say I preferred boxers," she told him in a careful undertone, aware suddenly, she was the only female in a room of rather gleeful men.

"You don't prefer boxers?" he asked with loud and devilish delight.

She felt her blush deepen. "I only said that because there is more of them. To eat. I don't have a preference in men's underwear. I mean if I did, I certainly would not discuss it with you."

He raised his eyebrows wickedly at her, and she realized she was just digging herself in deeper, much to everyone's enjoyment.

She shot him a snotty look, and then turned her attention to the cake. Despite having come out on the losing end of the undergarment discussion, Jessie marveled at the detail on it. There was a colorful icing patch, and the "hem" of one leg actually looked frayed.

"Want a piece?" he asked with wicked innuendo.

She looked at him. She had never met anyone like him before, so sure of himself, so engaging somehow, that even those—like her—who did not want to engage, were drawn in.

He stuck his finger right in the icing, licked it off, closed his eyes with approval. "You can put away the Tabasco, Clive, we won't be needing it."

She couldn't help herself. A little giggle escaped from her. She tried to muffle it. Oh, he wasn't funny! She mustn't let him think he was funny. He was juvenile and cocky and way too sure of his charms. But another chortle slipped by her guard.

And then he laughed.

And Pete and Ernie and Clive laughed. The dog began to howl.

And that's when Jessie's contained little giggle turned to laughter, too.

Once she started, it felt as if laughter had been trapped inside her for way too long. It felt like a dam bursting, merriment bubbling out. Jessie laughed until her face hurt. Not just at his sense of humor, but also at how fate had put her here, and at her own ridiculous whimsy—that she was going to let what was in that box determine her fate. An educated woman giving in to such superstitious, mystical nonsense.

Still, if she did go for that kind of superstitious mystical nonsense, what did it mean that the box contained edible boxers? How did that bode for her future? Did that mean she would end up drinking beer on the tailgate of a truck?

She realized, with a sudden sense of loss, that it wasn't about the beer or the tailgate.

It was about a man and a woman enjoying a simple moment because they enjoyed each other. Her laughter dried up, and she suddenly felt a terrible sensation of loneliness, as if somehow, with all the education and all the accomplishments, she had somehow missed something. The most important thing of all.

Nobody noticed her shift in mood, because Garner was cutting huge slabs of cake. Forget the formality of plates and forks. The cake was put on paper napkins and everyone just dug in. She knew she should protest the size of the piece he handed her, but she didn't. Maybe she hoped it could fill that sudden emptiness in her.

She hoped he planned to leave the cake out here. She was going to need quite a bit of it to fill the sudden hole in her soul.

She tried to shake off the mood, but questions niggled at her. When had her life ever been just plain fun like this? When had it become such a serious grind all the time? Why was an impromptu party at coffee time in the dismal front office of an auto shop proving to be more fulfilling than anything she had ever experienced at faculty functions? Were the functions she attended with Mitch just a tiny bit stuffy? Certainly nobody ever ate cake with their hands or had the neighborhood hound slobbering on their shoes!

Jessie realized if she was going to keep her sanity, she had to stop this. She had to quit finding fault with her former life! But a little voice within her insisted on pointing out that she had inadvertently labeled her real life her former life.

No one announced the end of coffee time, and so it was eleven before the guys had headed back to work, and Ernie and Bert had gone.

"Is this any way to run a business?" she asked Garner, looking at the clock and giving a little squeak of dismay.

"It's the only way to run a business," he said and ducked out the door.

Oh! But yesterday it had practically been a hanging offense when she'd been a few minutes late. But she was aware things had changed a great deal since yesterday, changed more than things should in such a short amount of time.

A moment later, while she was still contemplating the way he ran his business, a little magic mixed with the mechanics, Garner came back in. "I just need—"

"What?" she said when he stopped.

"You have something right there."

She cast a furtive look over her shoulder at her derriere. It would be too embarrassing if something was stuck there again!

"Not there." He crossed the tiny distance between them and touched the corner of her lip with his finger.

"Haven't we done this before?" she asked. Her voice came out as a very unattractive croak.

He stroked the delicate corner of her lip. She knew she should move, or tell him to stop, but she was paralyzed by sensation. Was it even possible that a touch that light, that unconsciously tender, could cause such a reaction? She felt weak with…something.

Wanting, her little voice within informed her helpfully.

His finger left her lip. He showed her the dab of icing he had removed, and then very slowly, his eyes never leaving hers, he put that dab of icing in his own mouth.

What little breath she had left felt like it was sucked right out of her. Her eyes were absolutely locked on the firm outlines of his lips.

He leaned toward her. For a panicky, exhilarated moment she thought he was going to kiss her.

"So, did you like it?"

She stared at him, dumbfounded.

"Eating my shorts?" he teased her, and then sauntered out of the room, but not before casting a knowing look back over his shoulder.

Good grief, he had known she would be watching him!

Well, that was because he was good-looking. He was probably an expert on women and the effect he had on them. He probably played with poor, unsuspecting women all the time! Even evil old Fannie had completely succumbed to his considerable charm.

It humiliated Jessie to be so predictable. It was humiliating to let him think he had any kind of power over her.

Did he have any kind of power over her?

She sank down at her desk. Had he almost kissed her? Was that her imagination?

What would she have done if he had kissed her, if he had leaned forward and taken her lips with his own? If her knees had gone weak from the tiniest touch of his finger, what would have happened if he kissed her?

Could she possibly be the kind of girl who would swoon? And if she was, how was it possible she had been such a stranger to herself for so many years?

Maybe this was what happened when a person leashed their passion too rigidly. And wasn't that what she had done, since she was fourteen, and, fresh from the pull and power of her own first kiss, had discovered the devastating secret of her mother's passion?

What would she have done if Garner Blake had kissed her?

"Slapped him, I hope," she said out loud, but she somehow doubted that was what she would have done at all.

What would it have felt like?

What would he have tasted like?

"Cake," she said quietly, trying desperately to be the pragmatic one.

It seemed to her, her life would have been so much simpler if that box would have just held roses from Mitch!

She went back to work more determined than ever to focus only on sorting out the mess that was his outer office, and determined not to think one more thought about his devastating lips. She was disciplined, after all.

No one went through six grueling years of university without developing discipline.

But suddenly it seemed as if nothing she had ever learned was going to be a defense against the blood of her mother, which she was suddenly aware, ran like fire through her veins.

Garner couldn't believe what had nearly happened in there. He'd spotted that delectable little piece of sugar and cream clinging to the corner of her delectable little lips, and he'd very nearly removed it...with his tongue.

The girl looked great this morning in her new duds. Who would have thought a girl with her kind of background would have looked so at home in a pair of jeans and a T-shirt?

Who could have known what an improvement it was over yesterday's getup?

Those curves she had so cleverly disguised yesterday were making themselves known today. The jeans hugged her in all the right places. They looked like they'd been melted onto the delicious curve of her fanny. And the T-shirt made her look round and soft and utterly gorgeous. Not to mention about ten years younger than she had looked yesterday.

"Garner, get a hold of yourself. She's a damn King. She wants to change her look, no problem. She goes and buys the jean store! She turns up her nose at tailgate parties!"

It was a reminder he couldn't just kiss her because he felt like it.

It was way more complicated than that.

Still, he couldn't help but wonder what she would have tasted like.

How she would have reacted.

He was willing to bet, from that soft, smoky look that had come into her eyes, that she would have kissed him back.

"Just before she slapped you silly."

Working with Jessie King was just a little too much like working with a stick of dynamite. Things were explosive between them.

Even if he *did* have a tailgate party with her, where did he think that would go? Oh, yeah, you had a beer, you looked at the stars, hands found each other and then lips.

And then the big explosion.

The kind that wrecked nice orderly lives like his.

At least with Kathy-Anne there had been no illusions. He had known damn well she was never going on a tailgate party. He had never even pictured her on one.

Now seemed like a very good time to remind himself of the treachery of Kathy-Anne.

She'd been sponsoring his high school project, where he took the kids everyone called marginal, and rebuilt and refinished a car with them. When he'd had enough of the demands of his high-maintenance relationship with Kathy-Anne—after about two weeks, when the initial thrill of looking at her had worn right off—she'd pulled the plug on the project. Thankfully, he'd managed to pull it back together. He'd even been nominated for Citizen of the Year, an award that would be handed out at the annual town fund-raiser next weekend.

He knew it was no accident that he was thinking of Kathy-Anne now, even though she was yesterday's news.

That experience was a reminder to him that rich girls played with people. They owned people.

They could change their whole look in a blink.

The phone rang. His private line. The caller was

another old-car aficionado. He'd found the sweetest little MG Midget in Houston, Texas. He'd pay Mitch to fly down and give him an opinion on it.

Mitch felt as if a hand had reached down out of the heavens and saved him. A few days away from the beguiling green of Jessica's eyes and the frosted temptation of her lips was exactly what he needed to clear his head.

"You can't leave," she told him when he announced his plans moments later.

See? She thought she owned him already.

"Actually, I can. I've already got one foot out the door." And dammit, he really shouldn't find the fact she was blushing endearing.

"I didn't mean because I'd—I'd miss you," she stammered defensively.

And his endearment deepened.

"I just meant I'm trying to learn a new job. It says here on the job description it requires constant supervision."

"It does?"

"You don't know what the job description says?" she demanded.

"Aunt Mattie wrote it. The guys will help you out. You know the most important things already."

"I do?"

"You know where the dog cookies are, and the cream. The coffee could use some work." He watched her face. "When your hand curls around the stapler like that, are you thinking of throwing it?"

Her hand moved instantly from the stapler. "Of course not!" she said with grave dignity.

Her flashing eyes said something else.

"Mmm-hmm," he said with disbelief, and smiled to himself when her hand crept toward the stapler again.

She seemed to realize it and moved both her hands firmly onto her lap.

"Well, at least give me a key," she said. "I'll come in late and try and figure things out when the phones aren't ringing and the guys aren't wanting a zillion things at once."

A key, he thought. So now a King wanted a key to his premises. Except they were also King premises. Still, she could be in there trying to dig up something for her father, but he didn't think there was anything to dig. There were no financial secrets, no dirty dealings, no under-the-table deals. So she could knock herself out in that department. Maybe her investigation would even lead to her figuring out the invoicing and inventory system.

Besides, if she was in on some sort of secret agenda for her father, she was a damned good actress, even for a rich girl.

"There's an extra key under the mat outside."

"Imaginative," she said dryly.

"And I'll give you my cell phone number. In case of emergency." Now why had he said that? He never gave anyone his cell phone number. He was trying to get away from her. To clear his head, to think! How was he going to do that if she called him, if that husky voice reached out to him in Texas?

"It's only for emergencies," he warned her as he grabbed a piece of paper off her desk and jotted down the number. "Flood, fire, famine."

She glared at him. "What did you think? I'd call if I broke my fingernail? Believe me, I'm not that anxious to hear your voice."

It was said just like a woman who was looking forward to a few days to clear her head, to think.

Chapter Five

Jessica slammed down the phone, then laid her head on her arms.

"Don't cry," she ordered herself, and then promptly burst into tears. It was ten o'clock Saturday evening. She was in the front office of K & B and thankfully she had it to herself. It was day six on the job, and her desk was emerging from under the rubble, especially since the auto shop was closed today, and she'd had the whole day to quietly sort things out.

No distractions, the main one being Garner Blake, who was still away. He had amazed her—and she suspected himself—by calling daily to see if she needed anything.

Okay, so his voice—deep, assured, unconsciously sensual—was a bit distracting, but not quite as bad as the real thing.

So the filing system was beginning to make sense. She was beginning to be able to decipher the mysteries of the Chilton Flat Rate Manual. She could order parts. She was getting pretty good at booking the right length of appointment. She was getting caught up on some simple accounting.

And each of her victories had just turned to dust.

Because that had been Mitch just now, not Garner. When Garner phoned, he asked if Bert was behaving himself, and if she'd seen Mrs. Klippenhopper. He teased her about mice and asked if she had eaten any shorts lately. *Then* he asked if there were any problems she needed help solving, or if she had any questions.

Mitch had phoned for the sole purpose of informing her that he had purchased a Slim Gym—for her. A Slim Gym was a much advertised piece of exercise equipment that looked frighteningly like a dentist's chair, only with more metal, pulleys and ropes surrounding it.

Instead of saying what she truly felt—that she didn't want a Slim Gym, and that she didn't need one, either, Jessie had said, "That won't fit in my apartment."

But Mitch had claimed it could fold up to fit under the couch.

She'd been willing to bet it would take more than their combined degrees in science to figure out how to make that happen!

"I guess I could keep the Slim Gym at my place for a while. Besides," Mitch had said, blithely unaware that she'd been sitting on the other end of the phone, hurt by his non-too-subtle message that he found her curves anything but glorious, "you won't be in your apartment much longer. We'll be married."

Fantasizing about a wedding was one thing, but setting a date was quite another. How soon was he thinking they were getting married? For some reason, she had assumed a long engagement, maybe because he had taken his sweet time about popping the question. Even when he finally had, she'd been shocked and unprepared.

Even though it was what she wanted most in the world. Wasn't it?

"Your apartment isn't any bigger than mine," she told him, striving for a tone that let him know how much she appreciated the fact he was thinking of her.

Why couldn't she just tell him she *hated* the Slim Gym without ever laying eyes on it? Why couldn't she be honest with her fiancé? She knew what she'd say to Garner if he ever made a boo-boo like the one Mitch had just made. It would be a short sentence, with a word in it that would make Mitch's ears turn red.

That's what a week working around men who were sweetly rough around the edges got you—a brand-new vocabulary.

But since Mitch would not appreciate the vocabulary, she tried to make him see things in a different light, as diplomatically as possible. "Are you really willing to sacrifice the aquarium in your apartment to accommodate the Slim Gym?"

For the first time he seemed to be detecting her lack of enthusiasm for his gift.

"We won't be living in my apartment for long," he finally said. "But maybe I'd better put a hold on the order until we move."

"Move where?" she asked, astonished. She loved his apartment, a cozy little scholar's retreat, crowded with books and old rugs and dusty collectibles. It was just a short walk to the campus from his front door.

"Well, Jessica, we'll be buying a house." This information was imparted in the genius-to-idiot tone of voice that he usually used only on the least gifted of his students. "I've been looking on the Hill."

The Hill was a bump in the landscape located well west of the university. It was, nonetheless, a bump well out of the price range of a college professor, or even two college professors. The brand-new homes there, built on an artificial hill surrounding an artificial lake, started in the half-million-dollar range.

What was he doing looking at houses without her?

"How would we be able to afford that?" she asked, instead of saying what she really thought, which was that she did not really like the Hill, or its brand-new houses. She liked old houses that dripped with charm and Virginia creeper. She liked trees that were a hundred years old, not a thing artificial about them. Coincidentally she liked neighborhoods just like the ones here in Farewell.

Mitch laughed, but it did not sound very sincere. "Couldn't we get it on your overtime? I did reach you at your office number, and it's late. Saturday night. How much did you say you were getting paid there?"

Why didn't he just say because her family was richer than the Hiltons? Had their communication always been this skewed?

"With your first check, we could get a yacht, too. We'll need it for the lake."

She wasn't sharing his sense of humor, especially since it seemed designed to make her feel small. He knew darn well what she was making since she'd made the mistake of telling him when she had first found out herself. Professors didn't make much, but they were kings compared to the salary she was making at K & B Auto.

Mitch was suddenly miffed that she wasn't enjoying his dig at her low wages.

"Jessie, get out of that godforsaken place and come home. You've only been there a week, and you aren't yourself anymore."

If he could see what she was wearing, he'd add *and how* to that statement.

Tonight it was a pair of flare-legged Lycra-infused black pants and a pink T-shirt that said Don't Say Farewell To Farewell, The Prettiest Town In Virginia.

She decided to take the advice on her T-shirt rather than her fiancé's, even though that did not speak particularly well of their relationship.

On the other hand, a Slim Gym? As a gift? And he was a man who was supposed to be smart!

"I'm not coming home," she said.

The word home felt like a foreign phrase on her tongue, as if she no longer knew what it meant or symbolized.

Jessie had a feeling she needed a little more time away from Mitch. Their worlds had been too closely intertwined for too long. Had she lost perspective?

"Jessica, I just don't understand what's gotten into you."

Cake shaped like underwear, for one thing.

"My father asked me to do this, and I'm doing it." There it was again, that funny dishonest twist in the communication. Why not just tell him she needed time?

"Well, it's a good thing your father subsidizes you, or you'd be starving to death."

So, he *was* really angry that she was saying they couldn't afford that house when he knew she got a very generous allowance every month from her father. Or maybe she was just being overly sensitive. Or maybe they were both having some premarital jitters.

"Maybe I should call your father," he'd said.

Good luck getting through. She had been trying to

reach her dad for over a week, and she kept hearing increasingly feeble excuses.

"That's rather patriarchal, isn't it?" she'd asked. "You and my father are going to decide what is right for me?"

Mitch had grumbled something incoherent.

"Mitch, I am a grown woman. I've decided to do this, and I don't want you treating me like a child, as if I can't make my own decisions."

There, she'd thought, pleased, *that was mighty clear.*

Mitch hadn't seemed nearly as pleased with her clarity. There'd been a long silence, and then Mitch had said, a trifle sulkily, "I guess I've acted as your advisor for long enough that I thought you trusted my opinion. I phoned to tell you I'd bought you a lovely gift, and somehow we're squabbling."

How was he managing to turn this around so that *he* was the injured party?

It's not as if she had purchased him a Slim Gym. Not that it would have hurt him to use one. A little paunch pushed against his classic argyle sweaters.

"I have to go," she'd said. It was true, she had to go. Before she said something rash and impulsive.

Such as *I can't marry you.*

Such as *I am not fat. I have glorious curves.*

Such as *take your Slim Gym and drop it off the roof of the science building.*

"Don't hang up," he'd said.

She'd hung up, laid her head on her arms and then burst into tears.

Then she remembered there was still some cake in the fridge, quite a large portion of it. She was going to eat it all, in defiance of Mitch's stupid Slim Gym.

She was sniveling so loudly on her way to the fridge

that she didn't hear the outer door open, and she nearly jumped out of her skin at the small diplomatic cough from behind her.

She whirled, her heart in her throat.

Seeing it was Garner, her heart really had no excuse to continue in double time.

"You're back," she said, then felt foolish, since it was obvious he was back. She had known he had to come back today, anyway. The town's annual fund-raiser was tonight, and Ernie and Clive and Pete were all so proud that Mitch had been nominated Citizen of the Year. They'd wanted her to go to the function, but she'd begged off, saying she would have felt out of place.

Now Garner looked absolutely amazing, in a beautifully cut black tux, the classic white shirt, the bow tie long since unknotted and hanging loosely around his neck. If he'd looked like a prince in a T-shirt and jeans, now he looked like a king.

Thankfully, he seemed unaware of her awed reaction to him.

"What's wrong?" he asked. She loved the expression on his face—warlike, as if when he found out who was responsible for her tears he was going to tear them to shreds.

It was primitive and a little thrilling. Still, she was not confiding in him about her fiancé's terrible lapse in judgment.

"Nothing is wrong," she said proudly, and scrubbed at her wet cheeks with her sleeve.

"Is this my fault?" he asked. He crossed the distance between them, looked down at her his eyes sparking with fierce intensity. "You should have said something on the phone if you were feeling overworked and underpaid."

"It's not that, exactly."

"Overwhelmed and underappreciated?"

"Well, a small raise…" she managed to croak, trying to make it about something it wasn't. More dishonesty.

Only, he didn't buy it. He touched a tear.

He really had to stop touching her. Not her lips, not her tears. Every part of her was off-limits. But did she say that? Oh, no, just closed her eyes and savored the strength and delight of that touch.

She opened her eyes to see him put her tear to his lips, and taste it with a kind of sensual reverence that should really be reserved for icing.

She gulped.

"How about a present instead of a raise? I brought you one," he said.

"You brought me a present?" *It'd better not be a Slim Gym.*

He slid something out of his pocket.

"What is that?"

"Now, that should be rather obvious to you."

"It looks like a little diamond tiara, like the kind you get at children's birthday parties."

"Exactly," he said, pleased, for some reason, that she had recognized his tacky offering.

With great care he settled it on her head. He rearranged a few strands of her hair.

His fingers in her hair in such an intimate and completely inappropriate way did the same thing to her that her tears on his lips did.

Turned her world upside down.

"I bought it at the fund-raiser. It's a tiara," he said, "for the only princess in town."

"Oh," she said. "That's ridiculous." Nonetheless she

Play the Lucky Hearts Game

and get...

2 FREE BOOKS

and a **FREE MYSTERY GIFT...**

yes! **YOURS to KEEP!**

I have scratched off the silver card. Please send me my *2 FREE BOOKS* and *FREE mystery GIFT*. I understand that I am under no obligation to purchase any books as explained on the back of this card.

Scratch Here!

then look below to see what your cards get you... 2 Free Books & a Free Mystery Gift!

310 SDL EFWW

210 SDL EFVM

FIRST NAME

LAST NAME

ADDRESS

APT.#

CITY

STATE/PROV.

ZIP/POSTAL CODE

(SL-R-06/06)

Twenty-one gets you
2 FREE BOOKS
and a ***FREE MYSTERY GIFT!***

Twenty gets you
2 FREE BOOKS!

Nineteen gets you
1 FREE BOOK!

TRY AGAIN!

Offer limited to one per household and not valid to current Silhouette Romance® subscribers. All orders subject to approval. Please allow 4-6 weeks for delivery.

BUSINESS REPLY MAIL
FIRST-CLASS MAIL   PERMIT NO. 717-003   BUFFALO, NY

POSTAGE WILL BE PAID BY ADDRESSEE

SILHOUETTE READER SERVICE
3010 WALDEN AVE
PO BOX 1867
BUFFALO NY 14240-9952

NO POSTAGE
NECESSARY
IF MAILED
IN THE
UNITED STATES

was delighted. She felt more like a princess than she ever had in her entire life. She tried to disguise her delight by frowning at him.

"Have you been drinking?"

"Not yet."

What did it say about this man that he could be so funny and natural without a drink? It said, she told herself sternly, he had way too much confidence in himself and his charms.

Mitch usually took at least three vodka twists before he loosened up a bit.

"You plan to start drinking?" she asked a bit hopefully. *Be flawed, Garner Blake.*

"Only if you'll join me on the tailgate of my truck."

She stared at him, aghast. She couldn't join him on the tailgate of his truck. She was an engaged woman.

Of course, she was engaged to a man who had just bought her a *Slim Gym!*

Besides, Garner was kidding, wasn't he?

The phone started ringing and she inadvertently cringed.

"You expecting a call?" he asked. He had not missed her tiny little flinch.

"No."

He reached for the phone.

"But if it happens to be for me," she said quickly, "I'm not here."

He raised an eyebrow at that, he scanned her tear-stained cheeks and then nodded, curtly. "It wasn't the job that had you in tears, was it, princess?"

Suddenly she couldn't lie anymore. When she didn't answer, a look came onto his face that would have made any man quell in his boots. He picked up the phone. "K & B Auto." His voice was formidably hard.

He watched her face. "Who? Oh, Jessica. No, she's not here." He paused for a long time, letting it sink in that he lied for her and that he didn't like it. But then, apparently he decided he was in it, he might as well do it right. Because he added, "I think she's in the hot tub with Roberto."

And then he hung up the phone and folded his arms over his chest.

She stared at him. She willed herself to be angry. He had just complicated her life unbearably. How was she going to explain that one away?

"How could you?" she asked. "My life is ruined."

"He made you cry," Garner said simply. "He's lucky he didn't come knocking on the door."

She gulped. "Would you have done something, er, barbaric?"

"Of course."

"That's awful," she said, but she was disgusted to discover she didn't mean it. "And Roberto? How am I going to explain Roberto? The hot tub?"

Garner shrugged. "He either trusts you, or he doesn't."

"He does," she said too quickly.

"Ah. But do you trust yourself, Jessica King?"

"Of course." But it was so weak she might as well have said no.

"It might be a good thing to find out right now."

"How?"

"Come on a tailgate party with me."

She wasn't sure if she could trust herself right now. Because his anger had faded and pure devilment shone in his eyes. She was wearing a tiara, and she was about to throw caution and decorum to the wind and go to her first tailgate party.

It should have felt all wrong, as if she was betraying Mitch and herself. But for some reason, it felt so right.

"You aren't dressed for a tailgate party," she said, a halfhearted last-ditch effort to stop this runaway train.

"How do you know what I'm dressed for?" he asked.

"I know the fund-raiser was tonight. And that you were nominated for top honors. Did you win?"

He rolled his eyes, embarrassed. "It's just a whole lot of small-town silliness."

"You won," she guessed.

"I liked buying the tiara better."

He had liked buying a toy tiara better than being elected Citizen of the Year? Who could resist a man like this?

It was just another small and corrosive dishonesty that she was pretending she could. She sighed, looked him in the eyes and nodded.

"Okay," she said, part resignation and part reluctant excitement, "a tailgate party it is."

Garner stared at her. He was very aware he was playing with fire—and loving it.

A tailgate party with Jessica King.

Okay, it was no doubt going to make his life unbearably complicated at some point, but he was going to choose to live for the moment.

And the moment was her—her green eyes huge, still shining with tears, those pants looking as if they'd been painted on, that shirt the color of passion and hugging her curves. And that tiara perched on top of her head as if she'd been born to wear it.

Besides, he hadn't liked the sound of the beau. There had been a little too much phony culture in that put-on accent. Garner knew it was much too harsh a judgment to make on such a short encounter, but he had made it anyway.

Headlights glanced off the front window and he turned to look and barely stifled a groan.

Who else would be in a chauffeur-driven white limo?

Kathy-Anne was disengaging herself. She was wearing a long red gown, sequined, and it hugged the hard angles of her fashionably skinny frame.

"Who is that?" Jessica asked as Kathy-Anne made her way to the door, stumbled, righted herself then launched at the door again.

"Nobody you want to know." *Nobody I want to know,* he thought. He wished he would have locked the door behind him. He and Jessie could have gone and hidden under the desk.

That probably would have been just about as much fun as the tailgate party. He slid her a look. Maybe more.

But it was too late. Kathy-Anne was sashaying toward him.

"Garner, where did you go? You left so early!"

"Yeah, well."

If Kathy-Anne noticed it was not a complete sentence, she didn't let on.

Her eyes had found Jessica, and she was focused on her now with a kind of predator-like intensity.

Garner felt furious protectiveness well up in him again. He wanted to place his body between her and Jessica. Kathy-Anne could be cruelly judgmental and not the least shy about sharing it, and he was not sure he could be held responsible for his actions if she said anything to hurt Jessie's feelings.

"Oh," Kathy-Anne said, looking at the tiara with stripping disdain, "you are?"

"This is Jessie King, my new office manager."

Kathy-Anne's expression altered, to one of concentration. "Jessie King," she said. "Do I know you? I never forget a face."

Except her own, Garner thought unkindly, which she painted into a brand-new expression every day.

"No, we haven't met," Jessica said coolly.

He looked at Jessie with interest. To his surprise she was not the least intimidated by Kathy-Anne. Mrs. Klippenhopper had nearly done her in, but she was not afraid of Kathy-Anne?

Well, why would she be? They shared a world where money mattered, and Jessica's family's wealth would probably put Kathy-Anne's substantial family fortune to shame. Besides, Jessie had more smarts in her little finger than Kathy-Anne had in her entire brain. And just because she chose not to look like Kathy-Anne didn't mean she couldn't, if she wanted to. Without even blinking, she could probably buy ten dresses like the one Kathy-Anne was wearing.

And Kathy-Anne seemed to suddenly realize that. She squealed. "That Jessie King! One of the King princesses. I saw your picture in *People* at your sister Brandy's wedding!"

Now Jessie was looking uncomfortable, her face remote.

"I love your sister Chelsea!" Kathy-Anne gushed.

"You know my sister?" Jessica asked.

"Not personally, but I would love to. She has the most incredible fashion sense!"

"So people say," Jessica said with a touch of dryness.

"Garner! You've been holding out on me. You didn't tell me you knew the Kings!"

He was never filling her in on that long and rather complicated story. "Who I know isn't nearly as important as what I know," he said.

Kathy-Anne rapped him smartly on the arm. "I hate it when you go all philosophical on me," she said.

"Well, if you two will excuse me." Jessica had her purse up over her arm and scooted out the door. She looked like a mouse who had escaped a cat.

And he suspected she did not consider Kathy-Anne, for all her claws, to be the cat.

"Wait!" he called.

But she didn't. He watched her go with regret and relief mixed in equal parts.

What had he been thinking? That Jessica King, one of the richest women in America, was going to go sit on a tailgate with him and sip warm beer and watch the stars come out?

Oh, yes, he remembered very clearly what he had been thinking.

That playing with fire would be fun.

Ha-ha.

"Garner—"

He took a deep breath, bracing himself. *Could we try again? Could we get back together? We made a mistake.*

But she didn't say any of those things. She said, "Do you think you could introduce me to Chelsea King?"

He glared at her. "No," he snapped, "I can't introduce you to Chelsea." He did not add that he did not know Jessica's sister, though like everyone else who subscribed to a newspaper, or turned on the TV every now and then, he'd seen her a thousand times.

"Close the door behind you," he said, brushing past Kathy-Anne. Dumb to chase Jessie down, but maybe he could salvage something.

But when he ran out into the night, Jessie had melted into the darkness. And since he could hear Kathy-Anne coming out behind him, he just kept running.

Sarah Jane MacKenzie was pretty sure no MacKenzie in the history of the world, or at least her part of the world, had ever been in a place like this.

The restaurant was beautiful—the linens crisp and white, the lights low, the tables and chairs an eclectic mix of antiques. A wall of windows looked out on the brilliant shimmer of New York City at night.

And across the table from her was Cameron McPherson. He was easily the best-looking man in the world.

His eyes were green, his hair burnished copper. He was wearing a dark blue suit and a tie, but she could tell that underneath it, he was all hard muscle.

She just knew she was going to embarrass herself, use the wrong fork, say something hillbilly, and he'd know who she really was, despite the fact Chelsea had made her over into a princess. And she didn't mean he would know she was Jake's granddaughter, either.

Sarah was learning a hard lesson sitting here in Chelsea's Allessandro Dell'Acqua cocktail dress and dripping jewels that Chelsea had referred to blithely as "bling." Sarah was learning that you could look like a princess all you wanted. But if you didn't feel like one, it was terrible.

And sitting here, looking across the table at the man of her dreams, a man she had felt she could love from the moment she had first laid eyes on him, she was terribly and dreadfully aware that she did not feel like a princess, even though she was Jake King's granddaughter.

And it was not because she did not know which fork to use.

It was because she knew herself to be a thief.

"Pardon?" she asked nervously. Chelsea, in a quick coaching session, had said it was better to say *pardon* than *what*.

He smiled at her as if she was charming and beautiful instead of gauche and unworldly.

"I asked how you came to work for Jake. There seems to be a bit of mystery around it. I'm supposed to be in charge of security, and no one seems to have an application with your name on it."

He was in charge of security, and she was a thief. It occurred to her, her life now contained all the elements of a fairy tale turning to a nightmare.

"You review every single application?" she said, evading his question. She hated the wide-eyed look she was giving him, as if she was a dumb bunny from the hills.

"No." He laughed. His laughter reminded her of a little brook she used to sit beside that gurgled down the side of a mountain, full of life and energy. "But after I met you at the wedding, I was curious about you."

"That's not fair," she said with an attempt at coyness, "to use your position to find things out about me. What could I have done if I wanted to find out things about you?"

He looked momentarily taken aback, and then he smiled. "Did you? Want to find out things about me?"

Everything: How old he was and what his middle name was and if he had ever thrown a fish hook in a stream. She wanted to know if he noticed flowers in springtime and what made him laugh and if he had a favorite movie and if he had ever felt so alone that he cried himself to sleep....

But she didn't say any of that. She only shrugged, trying for carelessness.

"So," he said, "let's get back to the application. None on file." He took a sip of his water—he hadn't ordered a drink—but the look in his green eyes was stripping.

Suddenly she wondered if this dinner was really about his interest in her.

Somebody had probably noticed things were missing from Jake's office.

Cameron probably didn't even like her. He was just pretending to be interested. Why would a man like that like her anyway?

"What's wrong?" he asked, and his hand suddenly covered hers. "Sarah?"

She looked at him, into the deep green pools of his eyes, and felt the easy and unconscious strength in his hands. She felt as if he was a man she could trust with everything, her every secret, her very soul.

"I just don't belong in a place like this," she said in a small voice. "Or with a man like you."

"Oh, Sarah," he said, and the sudden gentleness in his voice melted her. "Don't do that to yourself. Clint and I grew up so hard and poor the mice wouldn't have been able to find a crumb in our house."

She stared at him. "Really?"

He nodded, "Really. Now order the most expensive thing on the menu and enjoy it."

She whispered to him, "My menu doesn't have prices on it."

He laughed and whispered back, "It's the lobster. You want that?"

"Would it come with the shell on? And beady little eyes? And antenna? I saw that in a movie once."

"That's how it comes."

"Ugh. No!"

He laughed again, and she was almost able to convince herself that he really did find her refreshing and amusing.

Suddenly she knew what she had to do.

She just had to put back every single item she had taken from Jake. Then she would be worthy of the look she saw in Cameron's eyes. Relieved with her decision, she was able to relax for the first time since he had arrived at her door.

Chapter Six

Jessica took Sunday off. She was not risking any further one-on-one encounters with Garner where she might be talked into things she really didn't want to do. A tailgate party indeed. What had she been thinking to say yes?

At least when she spoke to Mitch, she was able to do so guilt free. She hadn't done anything. She explained to him that there was no Roberto and certainly no hot tub at K &B Auto. It was just her boss's idea of a joke.

"Ha-ha," Mitch said sourly. "So you were there with him, alone, at ten on Saturday night. I'm not sure how that's so different from being alone with Roberto."

No hot tub? she thought. But instead she said, "Look, Mitch, you either trust me or you don't."

Now she was quoting Garner. She was sure that wouldn't do, but on the other hand she heard amazing firmness in her voice. What she heard was *take it or leave it.*

Something was going dreadfully wrong with her engagement!

He must have heard it, too, because his tone suddenly changed. "Of course I trust you!"

She had managed to leave it on that note, before things deteriorated into a discussion of the Slim Gym or the house on the Hill, or before words popped out of her mouth that she could not take back.

Such as *I can't marry you.*

She had tried to reach her father, but James had told her he was out of town at a golf tournament. Supposedly it was first thing on his list to call her when he got back.

Her father was eighty-three years old. She thought it had been quite a number of years since he played golf, but what was she going to do? Accuse James of lying? Her father obviously wanted to avoid her right now. For some reason he didn't want her to know why he had sent her to Farewell, Virginia, or the details of how their family history was intertwined with that of the Blakes.

So she spent her Sunday holed up in her hotel room, determined not to think about her unraveling engagement, her fascination with a man who was not her fiancé or her father's mysterious desire to avoid her. She indulged herself in the only guilty pleasure that could completely take her mind off how surprisingly complicated her once-predictable life had become.

She read a romance novel, reading material that quite likely would have been scorned by her intellectual peers and certainly by Mitch. It was a delightful immersion in a wonderful fantasy. But when the last page was over, she felt curiously restless.

Could that kind of emotion and tenderness exist between a man and a woman? Was it out there somewhere? Or was it all an illusion? Why did reading a book like that make her feel so utterly hopeful and so utterly lonely at the same time?

She was the pragmatic King! She was marrying Mitch Michaels, a man she respected and liked and looked up to. She was looking forward to a life of stability, a reality far removed from the rarified air she had been breathing since she was a child. *But what about adventure?* a small voice inside her insisted. And a louder one asked, *What about love?*

Love! Didn't it wreck everything? Wasn't that what her mother had died for? Some flash in the pan with a younger man...

Jessica was sure she loved Mitch in a way. Just not *that* way. The way that made it feel as if you were standing on the edge of a precipice, your stomach hollow, your palms sweating, deciding whether or not to jump. Part of her wanted to be the girl who threw caution to the wind, who jumped off cliffs into the embrace of the unknown. And just as big a part of her wanted the absolute safety of a world unchanging: a comfortable easy chair, old books, a fire in the hearth.

So the next morning, after troubled dreams and with the two sides of her still very much at war, Jessie paired her new black pants with her old Chanel suit blazer. Underneath it she wore a white tank top that said, LLEWERAF—Look In The Mirror, Bub.

When Garner walked into her office, there was no mistaking which side of her personality was winning. He looked as gorgeous in a sky-blue T-shirt and worn nearly white jeans as he had in the tux.

She felt suddenly hot and had to discard the blazer.

"Yup, going to be a hot one," he said, regarding her with evil knowing over the top of his coffee cup. Then he looked at her chest for way too long, but that's what you invited when you wore clothing with backward messages printed on it.

"Where'd you run off to, Saturday night?" he asked. "I thought we had a date."

"I can't have a date with you," she said sharply, Jessie-of-the-easy-chair firmly in control. "I'm engaged to someone else."

She wagged her hand at him, her ring finger sparkling in the light.

Instead of being warned off, he stepped forward, took her hand and pretended to be studying the ring with grave interest.

Jessie-who-jumps-off-cliffs was about to get into the driver's seat if he didn't let go! But he did, stepped back from her and regarded her thoughtfully.

"So I guess he got over you and Roberto in the hot tub," he said.

"I guess he realized it was total malarkey."

"If that was my ring on your finger and somebody told me you were in the hot tub with Roberto, I would have been on your doorstep in a heartbeat."

"What about 'He either trusts you or he doesn't'?" she reminded him.

He shrugged. "Maybe there are some things you just want to see with your own eyes."

She hated it that he was making Mitch seem like some kind of failure, because he hadn't dropped everything and rushed to Farewell to rescue her from the imaginary Roberto. She hated it that she momentarily yearned for a man who would have done just that. Like the one standing in front of her.

"Hey," he said, taking another draw on the coffee, "this isn't half-bad, Jessie."

She hated that, too, that he could take her to that place rife with self-doubt and yearning and confusion, and then change the subject as if none of it mattered one little bit to him.

Which it didn't. Garner Blake was having fun playing with her life.

"Don't you have work to do?" she snapped at him.

"Yes, ma'am," he said, and the way he said *ma'am*, soft and drawn out, sensual as a touch, made her into Jessie-who-jumps-off-cliffs all over again.

He left, sauntering out of her office like a man who owned the world, and she braced herself for their next meeting.

It came at coffee time. The tension was there between them, a real and palatable force, despite the fact that they barely looked at each other. It was there as Garner was teased good-naturedly about being Farewell's citizen of the year. It was there, stronger, when Clive shyly brought out the pictures of his baby.

Jessie looked at that tiny wrinkled face and felt something inside her melt. She was introduced to an entirely new Jessie, not Jessie-of-the-easy-chair or Jessie-who-jumps-off-cliffs, but Jessie-wants-babies.

She felt stunned. She didn't want babies! She wanted a good education! A career! Maybe world travel for research purposes. Her and Mitch had that in common. No babies. They had discussed it on the way home from Brandy's wedding, where they'd been exposed to Clint's very energetic baby daughter, Becky. Jessie had been afraid to hold her. Mitch had said adamantly he felt he was too old for the lifestyle changes that would be required by a baby.

The picture trembled in her hand. Garner was staring at her as if he knew! As if he knew that just meeting him was changing everything about her well-ordered world, even her perspective on babies! She passed the picture back hastily and stood at the window, her back to them all.

Her mind was wiped clean of troubled thoughts by the sight coming down the main street.

"That woman is walking a pig," she managed to squeak, looking over her shoulder at her coworkers.

Clive chortled, Ernie sighed and Garner looked uneasy. Garner glanced out the window and something in his expression darkened.

"Hetta," he said when no one else said anything.

The woman was old and stooped, and she had a paper bag of groceries in one arm. The pig ambled beside her on a tiny leash that appeared to be purely decorative. Then without warning, right in front of K & B Auto, the bottom fell out of the grocery bag. Jessie expected a comic moment where the pig gobbled up the groceries, but it didn't happen. Instead the old woman sank down on the curb, looking distressed. The pig nudged her arm with his great snout and looked around.

If Jessie wasn't mistaken, the pig had his tiny eyes fixed on the audience at the window of the auto shop, and he was imploring them to help.

"I'll help her," she said, putting down her coffee.

Garner's hand stopped her, shoved her with gentle but firm strength into a chair. "Don't."

"But she's upset!"

The men were all studying their sandwiches and boots and coffee cups with intense interest.

"Oh, for Pete's sake," Jessie said and rose again. "I'll just be a minute. I think she's starting to cry."

The pig had his snout right on that wrinkled cheek as if he were trying to kiss away the tears that fell. The sight was in no way funny. It was heart-wrenching.

Again the hand restrained her. "Never mind. I'll go."

Why was he hesitating to help? Oh, wasn't that always the way? She thought she'd found a place that was old-fashioned and neighborly, where people still cared about each other and had values. Yet none of these men, even the one who was making her think renegade thoughts of babies, would voluntarily help that poor old lady.

"Not a great idea, boss," Clive said, taking a thoughtful bite of his sandwich.

But Garner's mind was obviously made up. He gave Clive a quelling look, stepped over the lunch boxes and went out the front door. It stuck open behind him.

"Don't close it," Ernie said. "There's no air-conditioning anyway, and I'd like to be able to hear."

"This should be fun." Clive adjusted his chair so that he had a better view out the window. He and Ernie and Pete elbowed each other and jostled for position with the enthusiasm of young boys about to see a schoolyard fight.

Obviously, Jessie noted uneasily, they knew something she did not know. She watched as Garner approached the old woman. He was behind her. He crouched and began to scoop her groceries and put them in a pile, since the bag was ruined.

"I'll just gather these up for you," he said quietly, his

voice deep and reassuring, the kind of voice one would use to gentle a frightened animal, "and then I'll find you a new bag to put them in."

The old woman glanced over her shoulder, initially pleased, and then her expression darkened when she recognized her rescuer.

"Here it comes," Clive said gleefully.

The woman reached for the nearest can, tomato soup, and threw it at Garner. He warded it off easily with his forearm and continued gathering her belongings, his expression grim.

"Clear out of there," Ernie suggested, though not loud enough that Garner could hear him.

Garner obviously felt once he started something, he had to finish. His face set in stoic lines, he focused on the spilled groceries.

"Get away from me, you young thug." The woman's voice was loud and commanding. Another can hit Garner.

"Spam," Ernie narrated.

The Spam bounced off Garner's leg. The pig was starting to look agitated. He shook his big pink head and pawed the ground with a surprisingly tiny foot.

"I bet that pig weighs four hundred pounds," Clive decided.

"Yep. Lots of bacon there," Ernie agreed.

Apparently neither of them were overly concerned that their boss was in danger of being run down by a huge pig.

"Get away!" the old woman shrieked furiously at Garner. "Hoodlum!"

"What's wrong with her?" Jessie asked nervously as she watched a package of noodles bounce harmlessly off Garner's head. "Is this town full of mean old women?"

"She's a King," Clive said matter-of-factly.

Jessie felt herself go very still. "A King?" She forced her voice into a monotone. "Does that mean something? I mean that's my last name, too."

"Oh, you ain't one of them Kings, or you never would have set foot in here. She don't even drive because she might have to get her car fixed here. How's that for stubborn?"

Jessie blanched. Was it possible she was related to this particular mean old woman? This feud nonsense was far more serious than Garner had let on. So why on earth wouldn't her father return her calls?

The exchange outside the window, though one-sided, was nevertheless becoming quite heated. It looked like the pig was backing up and preparing to attack. Garner, thankfully, had all the items that had fallen out of the bag now assembled in a sloppy pile.

He caught sight of the pig out of the corner of his eye.

"No!" he said, pointing a firm finger at the pig.

The pig hesitated and then sat down. Garner knew when to retreat. He stormed back through the door.

Clive grinned. "You got a way with pigs, boss. Who knew?"

"You can't just leave her sitting on the curb crying!" Jessie said.

"Yeah," Ernie said. "She's got a can of stew she ain't throwed yet."

"What do you want me to do?" Garner asked her, ignoring Ernie and Clive and Pete.

A memory was tickling Jessie's brain. Being a King princess, at Christmas they got a zillion gifts each, some of them from complete strangers. When they were little girls, year after year, they had always received three identical sweaters in garish colors with pictures knitted into them—one year a deer, the next a turtle. From Aunt Hetta in Virginia.

She felt sudden shame that she had never worn her gift from Aunt Hetta.

"Couldn't you drive her home?" she asked.

"And do what with the pig?"

"You have the company truck out there!"

He sighed. "Does she look like she's going to get in a truck with me? And even if she does, what if she starts throwing stuff at me while I'm driving?"

"Okay," Jessie said. "I'll drive her."

"No. I'm not letting you get in a truck with that crazy old woman. You don't know what she's going to do. Especially if she—"

He stopped and slid a look at the guys, but Jessie understood. Especially if she realized that it was her niece in bed with the enemy.

Not that she was in his bed. Good grief! Why had that phrase popped into her mind?

Still, she felt warmed by the fierce protectiveness on Garner's face. Not that she could allow it to control her!

"We could both do it. I'll drive. You ride in the back with the pig."

"You're kidding, right?"

She shook her head.

"Okay," he said, giving in suddenly and much too quickly. "But it'll cost you."

"What will it cost me?"

"Jessie King, you know very well what I want."

"What do you want?" she asked, and heard the shrill squeak in her voice.

"I want what I didn't get Saturday night."

The guys were nudging each other with pure masculine enjoyment now.

"I don't know what you're talking about," she said, tilting her nose upward.

He leaned very close to her. "You know what I want," he said, his voice as deep and as sexual as a touch.

"I do?" She tried for snooty outrage—and failed.

"You and me on a tailgate, baby."

"That's blackmail, you big oil ape."

He folded his arms over his chest. Out of the corner of her eye, she could see that Hetta was still sitting on the sidewalk crying, the pig making mournful, haunting sounds.

"I think you mean grease monkey, Miss MBA."

Ernie and Clive were looking back and forth as if they were at a Ping-Pong match.

"Okay, okay, whatever. You go get the truck and bring it around to the curb. I'll go talk to Hetta."

"Clive, you go get the truck. Jess, I'm not letting you talk to her alone. She's dangerous."

"She's old and she's addled. She's not dangerous."

"Yeah? Let's see if you still say that after you've been hit upside of the head with a can of Spam."

Jessie rolled her eyes at him, then retrieved a few plastic bags from under the counter before going out the door.

He flanked her like a warrior, though he stayed slightly back as she approached her aunt.

"Aunt Hetta," she said softly, "I'm just going to put the groceries in some new bags for you."

"I don't like plastic," she said querulously, squinting suspiciously at Jessie. "And who are you calling Aunt?"

"It's me, Jessica," she said. "You sent me sweaters for Christmas every year."

Bright eyes fastened on her face. Then an old hand reached out and touched her cheek with exquisite gentleness. "You're Jake's daughter? The middle girl?"

"That's right."

"Oh, my, aren't you all grown up?" Then she frowned. "The sweater I sent last year couldn't have fit.... Am I dead?"

"Excuse me?"

"Am I dead? Or having an 'allucination?"

"No. Daddy sent me to Farewell for a while."

Hetta's eyes slid to Garner. "Why are you with him?"

"I'm working for him."

"Humph, that sounds like plain bad medicine. 'Course, your dad's the crafty one. Probably has something up his sleeve."

"My thoughts exactly," Garner muttered. Hetta shot him an evil look. The truck pulled up at the curb.

"I'm going to drive you home," Jessie told her. "Garner's going with us."

"I'm not getting in any truck with him."

Garner sent Jessie the I-told-you-so look.

"He can ride in the back with the pig."

"Can't you take me by yourself?" Hetta asked. "Benjamin Franklin doesn't like strangers."

"She's not taking you by herself," Garner said, and Hetta apparently knew when to back down.

All four men, even old Ernie, helped hoist the pig into the back of the truck. Benjamin Franklin seemed to rather enjoy the attention; he was as regally happy with their arms locked together and straining under his bulk as an emperor on a chair being carried by slaves.

Garner looked less happy as he hopped into the back and sat on the wheel well.

The truth, Garner decided, was that his life had become insane since he'd met Jessica King. He'd eaten shorts, he'd paid fifty bucks for a child's tiara and now he was sitting in the back of his own pickup with a pig glaring balefully at him. Maybe this had been Jake's plan from the beginning. Maybe his daughter had a gift for looking so damned normal and dragging chaos in her wake.

He should have just given Jake the car.

Jessie was no Andretti with the clutch, either. The truck was pitching like a ship on rough seas.

It stalled without warning, sending the pig catapulting into him.

"Sorry," she called through her open window.

Her aunt was cackling happily.

He groaned; so did the pig. Garner moved off the wheel well, sank down on his rear and braced his back against the back of the cab. The pig regarded him out of those tiny eyes, and then groaned again, shuffled over and laid its head on Garner's lap.

As the truck lurched to a start again, Garner could only hope that pigs did not get sick.

Why was he subjecting himself to this?

A tailgate party with Jessica King.

Now *that* was insane.

Her aunt's place was on the edge of town, a neat collection of whitewashed chicken houses and her own tidy, ancient Cape Cod–style house. The garden was newly tilled and neatly weeded. It was a surprisingly charming little place, with its well-kept rows of vegetables and flowers.

The truck bounced to a halt, the pig buried its head deeper in his lap, trembling.

"It's okay. You're safe now."

Hetta came around back and called her pig, but the pig didn't move.

"He's usually a good judge of character, too," Hetta declared sourly.

"Well, the trip might have rattled him."

Jessie appeared at the back of the truck.

"Sorry," she said. She took in the scene solemnly.

Every time he tried to move, the pig burrowed deeper in his lap, pinning him.

"Can't you just push him off of you?" Jessie asked, uncertain.

"That's a lot of headcheese," Garner said. Nonetheless, he gave the pig's head a shove. It moved a fraction of an inch.

Hetta was looking pure hatred at him. She obviously didn't like her pig being referred to as any kind of food item made with pork.

"Benjamin," Jessie called tentatively. "Benjamin Franklin, come here."

The pig opened one eye and then the other.

She called again, and he fixed on her, found his feet and lumbered to the tailgate of the truck.

Okay, Garner thought, so it wasn't just him. Man and beast found her irresistible.

"Careful, he doesn't try to jump into your arms," Hetta said. "He becomes smitten and he thinks he's smaller than he is."

Somehow they managed to get the pig out of the truck, and Hetta, pig and groceries inside.

It was apparent to Garner that both the pig and the nasty old woman were smitten, because they couldn't leave until Jessica promised to return for tea. Then she and Garner got in the truck, with him, thankfully, behind the wheel this time.

He looked over at her.

She was smiling.

He couldn't help but smile, too.

"That pig was smitten with me," she choked out.

Then they were laughing, and nothing about his world seemed crazy at all. Garner liked being in the cab of his truck with Jessie. She had the window rolled down and the wind licked at the funny spikes of her hair. He took the long way back to the shop, strangely reluctant to arrive. When they did, he reached across her and opened her door.

"I'll pick you up at the hotel at nine," he told her.

"You aren't coming back to work?"

She asked this innocently, as if she had no idea that a man could lose his mind totally around her.

"No, I'll see you at nine."

He went home. Behind his house was an old stable that had been converted into a four-bay garage. In it were his treasures: the Silver Ghost that Jake was so determined to have, his current project, the sweet little Mustang, and his baby. The '45 Chevy truck was the first restoration project he'd ever done. He took the dust sheet off of it, ran his hands lovingly along the deep blue powder coat of paint.

He'd found the truck in a swamp when he was sixteen, a rust bucket, little more than the frame. He'd bought it for ten bucks, the farmer just happy to have it hauled away. It had taken him nearly two years to fix it up—to find or manufacture parts, to get every detail just right according to pictures he had acquired and magazines he was reading.

The first day he'd taken it out, he'd been offered twenty thousand dollars for it. A princely sum, more money than his family was seeing in a year at that time in his father's downward spiral of self-destruction, gambling, women, booze. His father had been furious with him when he'd refused to sell it. But Garner had known then, there would be other old vehicles that he would be able to work on and sell strictly for profit. Though the truth was he did fall in love with each of his finds, just a little bit.

Still, other tough times had come and gone and he still kept the old Chevy. He loved it, pure and simple. It had opened a whole world to him.

And he couldn't think of a better vehicle to have a tailgate party with.

Chapter Seven

Jessica stood nervously in the lobby of the hotel. It was ten to nine. She decided that if Garner was even one minute late it would be a sign that she was not supposed to go.

Of course, she already knew she shouldn't go. Mitch was still mad about the Roberto thing. In fact, things between her and Mitch seemed terribly strained. And now she was going on a date with another man.

Well, not really a date, she told herself. Garner had helped her with her aunt. This was the price she had promised to pay. A date would be a complete betrayal of her fiancé. Saying thank you to Garner for a good deed—keeping a promise she had made to him—was a good thing, a reflection of her own character. Garner, after all, had kept his promise to eat his shorts.

She realized her efforts to build a case for her honor had an almost-frantic quality. The truth was she suspected she was doing something she shouldn't be doing.

On the other hand, Mitch had all kinds of acquaintances and colleagues of the opposite sex that he met for the occasional lunch or drink after work. He said it was a sign of a mature relationship that she did not feel jealous. Then again, did Mitch feel like this before he left for those appointments? Excited, on the very edge of discovery?

She tried to remember if she had ever felt this many butterflies in her stomach.

Prom? First degree? Brandy's wedding?

No, she remembered feeling sort of this way only once before. A long, long time ago. She'd been fourteen and a boy named Dusty Tilsman had kissed her. She had felt as if she had been introduced to a world so thrilling she could not have guessed it existed. A world of pure feeling, a world ruled by laws that had nothing to do with her mind.

But at that same time, guiltily curious about the silence in her house surrounding her mother, and the circumstances of her mother's death ten years before that, she had done some research. She had only been four when her young mother had died and she had no conscious memory of the event. Jessica had found out what no one else seemed to know, though perhaps they all suspected it.

Perhaps because she was still reeling from the power of her shared kiss with Dusty, Jessica understood the force that had pulled her mother away from her children, from a husband forty years her senior, from all the rules of her world.

Dusty was immediately dismissed from Jessica's life. As were all things passionate. Jessica King was terrified that a wild child hid within her waiting to claw its way out and destroy her world as surely as her mother's had been destroyed.

Now Garner Blake was rekindling desire, curiosity, a longing for something…glorious. The look in his eyes, his every casual touch, the sound of his voice—they all beckoned to her, called to her to stretch her wings and fly, the way she had known she could since she was fourteen.

She shook herself out of her thoughts, glanced at the clock.

Five minutes.

She hoped he wouldn't come.

And knew she would die if he did not come.

Headlights glanced off the hotel's big picture window, and then the most beautiful truck she had ever seen rolled to a smooth stop in front of the hotel.

She gazed at the vehicle, awed. It was very old, with lovely round lines on the fenders and the cab. It had hardwood running boards, hardwood panels around the box. It was a color of midnight blue she was not sure she had ever seen before.

Garner Blake got out of the driver's side. His stride long and purposeful, he came up the walk. She felt frozen. If she took one step toward him, her whole world was going to change forever.

He paused in the doorway, scanned the lobby, saw her and smiled.

It was such a captivating smile—boyish, honest, welcoming.

He held out his hand.

She took that one step toward him and then another, but it didn't feel as if she was walking. She was floating on air. Flying.

"You look great," he said.

She glanced down at herself. Jeans, rolled up to her calf, a T-shirt that said Where In Hell Is Farewell? and a zipper-front, hooded jacket.

"You do, too," she said, and then blushed.

Because he only looked like himself—jeans, white T-shirt, that princely way of walking the earth, as if he owned it.

He helped her into the truck. It was exotic and masculine, leather and polish. Despite the fact the interior was probably years older than her, everything looked brand-new, buffed and lovingly restored.

"I love this truck," she breathed. "What is it?"

"A 1945 Chevy. I knew, in your heart, you were a truck kind of girl. A tailgate-party kind of girl."

It was getting dark as they drove through the tree-lined streets of Farewell. Kids cherishing the last light played football, lights winked on in houses with porches, somewhere in the distance a lawn mower engine cut and died. A young couple walked down a street, eating ice-cream cones, each with one hand on the baby stroller they pushed in front of them.

Life seemed simple, and Jessica felt a strange longing well up within her.

A few minutes later Garner turned into the driveway of a big house, white with green shutters, two stories, a porch wrapped all around it. It was like a house out of a dream—a place where a real family would live. A place where lemonade would be poured on hot summer nights and where chicken would roast in the oven on Sunday afternoons, where kids would play hide and seek in the overgrown lilacs that flanked the porch, where a baby would be safe in its bassinet on that wide, screened porch.

The aching in her throat was raw. "Where are we?"

"My place."

She should have known, somehow, he would live in a place like this: old-fashioned and reassuring. But she hadn't.

She had thought he would live in some nondescript little bachelor pad.

"We're having a tailgate party at your place? Somehow I pictured a deserted country road or a swimming hole or something."

"Don't worry. We aren't stopping just yet." He took a rutted driveway past the house, and they bounced past what looked to be old stables. Beyond the stables, the yard opened up. Once it had probably been a pasture. At the center of a field of swaying grass, woven with wildflowers, was a pond, with a weeping willow draping its fronds in the water. A frayed rope hung from one of the gnarled branches, as if a long time ago, children had swung, screaming, over the water.

"It used to be my grandfather's property. I was able to get it back a few years ago."

The ghost of the boy he had once been clung to that rope, laughing. The vision popped as Garner hopped out of the truck. Without waiting for him to open her door, she hopped out, too.

He opened the tailgate, spread a blanket on it, pulled a wicker picnic basket close. And then he turned, put both his hands around her waist and hoisted her up as if she weighed nothing.

Of course, to her amazement, when she had weighed herself this morning she had weighed five pounds less than when she arrived. Perhaps happiness did what no Slim Gym could ever do.

Was she happy?

The answer, at this moment? Blissfully.

"Is that a real pond?" she asked.

He gave her a quizzical look. "There's another kind of pond?"

"You don't know the half of it," she muttered, thinking of the artificial lake that was central to where Mitch suddenly wanted to buy a house. "Why did you choose here for our tailgate party?"

"It's pretty," he said. "It's private."

Oh-oh. What did that mean? That her loyalty to Mitch was going to be tested yet again? Why did they need privacy?

"And," he said softly, "it's one of my favorite places in the whole world."

She looked out over the pond, touched he would bring her to a place that was so special to him.

Garner hopped up on the high tailgate with ease. He didn't sit right beside her. The picnic basket was between them. She shouldn't be disappointed by that. She was engaged! To someone else. If her mettle was tested, she was pretty sure she would flunk. Just like her mother had.

"Don't frown," he said. "You aren't doing anything wrong."

But she thought she probably was.

He popped the lid of the basket. "What would you like? Coke or 7UP?"

"I thought you drank beer at tailgate parties," she teased, trying to rise above the war going on within her. Who was she, anyway? Pragmatic, passionless Jessie whom everyone could rely on? Or someone else altogether?

He looked at her, and the look was so smoldering her toes curled.

"Well, here's the thing, Jessie King. If you let me steal a kiss a little later, I don't want you saying it was the beer. I want you to know exactly what you're doing."

She went very still.

"I can't kiss you, Garner. I'm going to marry another man."

"Well, you aren't married to him yet."

"I promised. That should mean something. I don't even think I should be sitting here. Not with you."

"Why's that, Jessie King? Are you feeling something a very proper engaged lady shouldn't be feeling?"

As if she would admit that to him!

"Because if you are," he said, his voice low and seductive, as velvety as the darkness closing in around them, "now would be a good time to find that out."

She snorted, though her heart was hammering crazily. "And kissing you would help me find that out?"

He nodded.

"That's very egotistical."

He shrugged. "Maybe. Coke or 7UP?"

How could he change the subject like that? Probably because a stolen kiss would mean no more to him than the choice of a soda pop. She took the Coke, but she was aware her skin felt like it was shimmering, taut with the most exquisite tension.

"So who was the woman in the limo the other night?"

He opened a bag. "Pork rind?" he asked. "In honor of Benjamin Franklin?"

Despite the fact that he had not answered her questions, she laughed. They ate pork rinds and sipped Cokes.

"Her name is Kathy-Anne. I met her last year. She saw this house, actually, and wanted to buy it. A summer place in the mountains. We saw each other a couple of times. I was trying to launch a project for some high school kids—the ones they call marginal. I had found an old truck, something like this one, and I thought they could work on it, auction it off at the end of the year. Kathy-Anne offered to sponsor the project.

"Then she thought she was going to own my life. Rich people can be like that. They own things. When I let her know I wasn't going to be owned, controlled, bossed around or changed into the man who would escort her to the latest charity ball, she pulled her sponsorship. The whole thing almost sank, but I managed to finance it a different way in the end. She's bought so much in her life, she just can't get it that she can't buy me."

"Not all rich people are like that."

"Yeah, well quite a few are."

"I'm not."

"It's true that you aren't what I expected. But who knows, the other shoe may still fall."

She slugged him on the arm. "Be careful or *your* shoes might fall. Right into that pond."

"Okay," he said, "I consider myself warned."

When the pork rinds were finished and they had both started another soda, Garner reached back into the basket and pulled something out.

Then he moved the basket and scooted over beside her.

His leg was touching hers.

She knew she should pull away but she didn't. She kind of liked that shimmering feeling on her skin, and it intensified as the hard muscle of his leg touched hers.

"What's that?" she asked.

"The only bubbly you're going to see tonight," he said.

He unscrewed the lid of the bottle and removed a wand. He blew on it. A perfect, huge iridescent bubble floated out over the dark water, hung for a moment, then floated down and popped.

He blew again, and this time a series of bubbles, translucence outlined with pinks and purples and blues, floated out over the pond.

He turned and looked at her.

She was looking at his lips. Blowing like that shaped his lips almost the very same way they would shape right before he kissed somebody. He winked at her, handed her a bottle of soap, and soon, she was laughing helplessly as she competed with him. Biggest bubble, most bubbles with one blow, longest-lasting bubble.

She became aware of how comfortable she felt. She considered the possibility that it was the very first time in her life she felt as if she was not pretending, not trying, not on trial. She was not one of the King princesses. She was not the protégée of the science department. She just was. A feeling of complete contentment crept over her. Which was why she allowed his hand into hers, warm and strong and sure. The laughter died, and the stars winked on.

"Can I kiss you now?" he whispered.

The feeling of contentment popped as surely as those bubbles they had blown.

She decided on honesty. "I'm afraid."

"Why?"

"Because I'm engaged."

"That's not why you're afraid."

"It isn't?"

"You're afraid because I might make you feel something he doesn't."

She squirmed uneasily and jerked her hand out of his.

"One little kiss, Jess. It could tell you everything you need to know."

"Or something I don't want to know," she said.

"Why are you so afraid to know who you are?"

"Do you really want to know?"

"Yeah, I really do."

Then it was all coming out. She was telling him all about Dusty and her mother, and suddenly she was sobbing helplessly.

He didn't say a word. He gathered her in his arms and held her. The night turned chilly around them, but she did not feel cold. She felt as if she could trust him.

"Just for the record," he said, "bad mothers don't make their children into bad people. Mine left when I was twelve, when all the money was gone and she realized the good old days weren't ever coming back. She was from a wealthy family in Charleston."

"Didn't she want you to go with her?"

"Nah. She left the whole thing behind, including me, as if it had been a bad dream."

"You didn't deserve that."

"And you didn't deserve a gold digger for a mother who married a man three times her age and then couldn't live with the consequences."

"How do you know all that?" she asked.

"Hey, I was about ten when your mother died. The whole world talked about it."

"Except my world," she said sadly.

"Jess, it's what life dealt you. And it hurt. But you know what? A little hardship in that rather privileged life you've led probably wasn't a bad thing. You aren't like any rich girl I ever met before."

Jessie had never heard her mother described so

bluntly. A gold digger? She wanted to rise to her mother's defense, and then she let it go. It was true. What he had said about her mother was true. And what he'd said about *her* was true, too. Her mother's scandalous life had made Jessie reach for integrity, search for something more real than the glitz and glamor of her father's great fortune. She felt as if she had searched and searched for the place in the world where she fit. But if her search for integrity had been successful, why was she here?

Then he tilted her chin with his fingers, and she looked into eyes made inky dark by the night.

"Now?" he whispered.

Even though she willed every single fibre of her to say no, she did not.

She whispered, "Yes."

And Garner Blake kissed her.

Not with dominance, not with runaway passion, not with any male agenda that she could detect. He kissed her with exquisite tenderness.

His lips, without saying a word, spoke her soul's name. His lips beckoned to some part of her that had been hiding, telling that part of her to come forward.

When she answered him it was with that part of herself, long suppressed, that was her fire and her life, her spontaneity, her heart.

It was the part of her where reason was suspended.

It was not evil. It didn't need to be fought. Not at all. It was the part of her that had wings.

He pulled away, his eyes scanning her face, his thumb scraping the delicate swelling of her lips.

"Did that tell you something you needed to know, Jess?"

"I don't know," she whispered, but they both knew

it was a lie. "Tell me why things are so wrong between our families," she said after a while.

"What did your father tell you?"

"He's avoiding me. Trying to get through to him when he doesn't want to be gotten through to is like trying to break into a Pentagon computer. It can't be done."

"He and my grandfather, Simon, were the best of friends. They started Auto Kingdom together."

"They did?"

"It wasn't called that, then. It all started at that little garage right over there on Main Street. King and Blake Auto."

"But what happened?"

"I guess that depends who you ask. My grandfather would never say anything abut it. My father wouldn't shut up about it. How we'd been cheated out of what was rightfully ours by your father. I grew up believing Jake King was the worst villain in the world. We lost everything. Even this house for a while. I was able to buy it back a few years ago."

Jessie could feel a pain squeezing in her chest. This man had grown up hating her father! "I'm so sorry," she said. "I'm sorry if my family did do anything to cause you pain."

"It's kind of like the bad mother thing," he said. "Being poor was way better for my character than being rich. Having to work and finding what I love to do—restoring old cars—was a blessing, not a curse."

Despite the words, did she hear faint bitterness in his tone? She realized she had told Garner about her mother and her sister. She had given him things he could use to hurt Jake very badly.

"Those things I told you tonight…"

Something went cold in his face.

"Either you trust me or you don't," he said.

"Garner, I hardly know you."

"You can't kiss a man like that and then claim you hardly know him."

"Maybe it's myself I don't know very well," she said.

But whatever it was, she could tell by the look on Garner's face that this was one party that was over.

Garner could tell she regretted confiding in him. He decided it was a good thing he'd decided not to give her the beer.

Who knows what else he would have heard?

Maybe some juicy tidbits about the boyfriend…

The evening was spoiled by her regret. He knew what had happened. She had held that stuff inside her way, way too long, and at the first sign of a safe port, she unloaded it.

Good God, was he her first safe port since she'd been fourteen?

He sternly quelled the sympathy that tried to rise up in him. No! She might as well know what it felt like to have said things she didn't want to say. He had been filled with that very same regret from the day he met her. He just kept doing one foolish thing after another, as if he were a magnet, being drawn helplessly to her steel.

If there was a word he could not tolerate, it was *helpless!* Yet that was what he had been against her charms.

At least he was not alone. Everyone who met her seemed to come under her spell: Clive, Ernie, her impossible aunt, even the damned pig fell in love with her! The realization was like a light coming on. Suddenly he knew why her father had sent her.

Jake King was shrewd and manipulative, but subtle. He had known the devastating effect his daughter had on people. He'd known after a little time spent with her, she'd only have to blink longingly and the car would be hers.

Garner Blake decided to tip his hand. The question wasn't whether she could trust him, after all. The question was whether he could trust her.

"Do you want to see my car collection?" he asked casually.

"Is this anything like looking at your etchings?"

Damn, she was good. He braced himself not to be charmed.

Instead he silently packed up the picnic basket and helped her down from the tailgate. He tried very hard not to notice how she tipped her head back and looked up at the stars, gazed for a moment at the willow trailing its long fingers through black water, as if she was trying to memorize this moment.

He showed her the Mustang first. She loved it. She insisted on sitting in it and made him play the radio so she could be sure it worked. Again, he could feel the pull of her, of that enthusiasm, that life force, peeking out from her like sun peeking out from behind clouds.

He led her to the next bay. It was in darkness and he pulled the dust cover from the car and waited until she was inside before he threw on the powerful overhead light.

He watched her face.

Her eyes widened, her hands flew to her cheeks. Her mouth opened, but not a sound came out.

"Oh my God," she said. "I have never seen anything so beautiful. What is it?"

So Garner could be fairly certain her father had not discussed the car with her. Yet.

"It's a Rolls-Royce Silver Ghost Oxford Open Tourer," he said, and could not keep the pride out of his voice. "Circa 1923."

She walked to it slowly, ran her hand along the ridge of the driver's door. The look on her face was entranced, totally enchanted. If things were not so damned complicated, he would have sworn he had found the woman of his dreams. No one looked at an old car like that. Except maybe him.

"Come on," he said after a moment. "I'll take you home."

She looked reluctant to leave the car. All the way out the door she kept looking back at it. "What do you do with a car like that, Garner?"

A weak man would have probably just given the damn thing to her!

"I'll sell it eventually. It's posted on the Internet now." *Which is how your dad found it.*

"I do the restorations as a business, a sideline to K & B." He didn't tell her his earnings at his "sideline" outstripped what he made at K & B by a country mile.

"It must break your heart to sell a car like that."

He wasn't talking about broken hearts with her. "Two hundred grand takes the sting out a little bit."

"Mercenary."

It was more like *real world* but he didn't say it. What was the point? He already knew their worlds were miles apart, knew that it would be best if this thing didn't go any further. She'd kissed him back, but then she'd questioned whether or not she could trust him.

That thing happened again—words spoken that the moment they were out of his mouth he wished he could yank them back—just outside her hotel.

He'd said good-night. He had managed, by some miracle of self-control, not to kiss her after he'd walked her to the door and held it open for her. He decided it would be safest to leave her in the lobby. There was no telling when his mighty effort at control would snap, especially if she invited him into her room.

"Jessie!"

She was halfway across the lobby, and she spun and looked at him.

Her eyes said she would invite him in.

And his heart told him she wouldn't be able to live with herself after.

"You want to go for a spin tomorrow? In the Ghost?"

She ran back across the lobby and threw herself against him. She covered his face with little kisses while she said yes, over and over again.

How could a man keep his guard up around something like this?

"Okay," he said, putting her away from him, because his control was like an elastic band being stretched way beyond its breaking point, "I'll take that as a yes, then."

When she looked embarrassed, he turned away quickly, before he was fool enough to try to make that right, too.

Chapter Eight

Sarah Jane's heart was in her throat. She had never been so frightened in her whole life. When she had taken these items from Jake's office, one by one, she hadn't felt frightened at all, but exhilarated, *entitled.*

But putting back her little stash of treasures was a different story.

After her date with Cameron, when she had looked under her bed, Sarah had been stunned by how much stuff she'd acquired—three pens, a candy dish, a bud vase, two silver candlesticks, a tie pin and an antique book.

It was horrible. What had she been thinking?

She had been thinking it was okay, that's what she had been thinking. She had been thinking that since she was Jake's granddaughter, even if she was the only person in the world who knew it, she was entitled to something from him.

But looking at the stolen goods now, she felt sick to her stomach.

She wasn't just a thief. She was a liar. She should have told Jake the truth long, long ago. She should have trusted that her grandfather would do the right thing by her.

She snorted. Not that there had been a whole pile of people in her life who had ever done the right thing. But she couldn't make this about other people. It was about her. Sarah Jane should have trusted that she could handle it if Jake King, her grandfather, didn't welcome her into his family with open arms.

She hadn't handled things very well so far, but that didn't mean she couldn't change all that now. It was never too late to do the right thing.

She was putting her ill-gotten gains back, tonight, before her actions stole any more of her soul. Then tomorrow she was telling Jake that she was Fiona's granddaughter. His granddaughter. His flesh and blood.

She put all her stolen items in a cloth designer bag that Chelsea had given to her. With each item she placed in the bag, it felt as though a weight was lifted from her, as if she was light again, alive again, worthy of all life had to offer.

Maybe even worthy of what she had seen in Cameron's eyes.

He liked her. She knew he did. With time, with a chance, could it turn into more than liking? She shivered at the thought.

With that hope buoying her resolve, Sarah moved stealthily across the courtyard and through the back door of the big manor house. It was evening, and there were lots of people around, so none of the doors had been locked, but the office would be empty.

In fact, Jake had not come to the office today, and just thinking about how pale and tired he'd looked over the past few days made Sarah feel afraid.

She scooted down long hallways until she came to the office. No James, thank God. She opened the door and slid in. She wanted to just dump the bag and run, but of course, she couldn't. She had to put every single item back in a way that made it look as if it had never been missing in the first place.

Her heart hammering in her throat, she picked the pens out of the bag and slid open the top drawer of Jake's desk. It sounded so loud, like scraping metal. Next, she put the empty bud vase on a shelf behind his desk. The candlesticks went above the mantle.

The door opened just as she was about to set down the second candlestick.

Sarah whirled, the candlestick in her hand. When she saw James standing there, she shoved the silver behind her back.

Then she saw Cameron was behind him.

James crossed the floor swiftly and grabbed her wrist cruelly, dragging her hand out from behind her back.

"Just as I suspected," he said in the cool, oily voice that she had come to hate.

She looked past his shoulder. Cameron was looking at her. He folded his arms across his chest, as if he needed to protect his heart from her. The look on his face was momentarily stricken, but he quickly masked whatever he was feeling. His features looked as if they had been cast in stone.

James took the candlestick from her limp hand, spotted the bag. He went over to it and pulled out the tie pin and the book.

She stood with her head hanging, trembling.

"Just starting your evening's work?" James asked, his voice as cold as a flash-frozen fish.

"I—I—It's not how it seems." She said it to Cameron, not James. She glanced at him imploringly. She could say she was bringing it back, but who would believe her?

She could tell them—no, not James, but Cameron—who she was, and why she had done it. When she glanced at Cameron's face, even though it was cast now in steely remoteness, she saw some pain flicker in his eyes that made her think that he wanted nothing more than to understand.

But when James said it was time to call the authorities, her tongue stuck to the roof of her mouth. And then Cameron came all the way into the room and looked at the bag James was proffering. She knew how much tension he was holding when she saw his shoulders droop, just for a moment, before he straightened them again.

Suddenly all Sarah could see was the light of the doorway shining over one of those broad shoulders. She bolted for it.

"Get her!" James cried.

"Let her go," Cameron said wearily, and even took a step out of her way. "Just let her go."

She ran mindlessly out of the house. She did not even stop at her apartment. Nothing in it belonged to her anyway. It was charity from Chelsea and from Jake, people who had been so good to her. They had treated her like family, even when they had no idea that she really was.

She had turned on them like a junkyard dog.

She felt in her jeans pocket. There was a bit of money in there.

She wound up in the trees, by the break in the fence, and she knew she was leaving the same way she had come in. She stopped, briefly, gasping for breath, and counted what she had in her pocket.

Just enough to get her back to Virginia.

When she had first come here to Kingsway, it had been in a soaking rain. Now it was tears that soaked her face as Sarah Jane MacKenzie left Jake King's estate, her heart broken…by herself.

Jessie threw herself on her hotel bed. She rolled over and contemplated the ceiling.

She had just covered Garner's face with kisses, flung herself at him like a too eager puppy. Well, she was rattled. Not herself since that meeting of lips. She had kissed him, she had told him her whole life story, she had contemplated inviting him up here!

"You've lost your mind," she muttered to herself, but she was aware her muttering was without censure. She *liked* how she was feeling, as if life was brimming with possibilities, potential for almost anything to happen.

He'd asked her out again! To go in that amazing car with him. There was no reason for her to say yes this time. She was not keeping a promise. It was not about honor and character. But, oh, how she had said yes! Flung herself at him shamelessly.

She went very, very still. She even stopped breathing, wanting nothing to interfere with her sudden clarity of thought.

She was falling in love with Garner Blake.

It was impossible. Crazy. *True.* It was just about the truest thing she had ever felt.

Jessie knew, suddenly and with deep certainty, what she had to do. She knew what she should have done days ago.

She picked up the phone. "Hi, Mitch. Yes, I know it's late. It's important." The words she needed to say came out smoothly, as if she'd been rehearsing them all week.

Mitch was silent for an uncomfortably long time. Then, his tone clipped, he said, "You're being very impulsive, Jessica."

"Is impulse always a bad thing?" she asked gently.

"You're a scientist!"

How strange that the man she had agreed to marry would see that first—that she was a scientist. Not a woman, a lover, a soul mate, but a scientist. Of course, why wouldn't he? That's what she had always shown him—control, measured responses, logic.

"Love is not a science," she said out loud.

"You can't just phone me and call it off. We need to talk about it."

It had always been about what he thought, what he wanted. It had always been about winning his elusive approval. "I don't want to talk about it," she said firmly. "Goodbye, Mitch."

She felt free as she gazed at the phone. His reaction to their breakup had been an all too accurate reflection of the relationship. It had been about control rather than connection; it had contained way too much logic and predictability and not nearly enough emotion or passion.

"Goodbye, Mitch. Hello, Jessie!"

Then she phoned Kingsway. She needed answers. She needed to know the whole story, what exactly she was up against. "I need to talk to my father," she said.

James sounded distressed. "He took a sleeping pill a short time ago and went to bed."

"My father took a sleeping pill? Dad hates drugs! James, what is wrong?"

"We had a robbery here tonight. He's very upset."

"A robbery!" Jessie felt her heart fall through the floor. She'd been out kissing a man she had no right to be kissing on the tailgate of his truck, while that had been going on? "Is anyone hurt? Do I need to come?"

"No, no, it wasn't an armed robbery. A young girl your father hired was looting his office."

"Sarah," she said slowly. "I remember her from the wedding. I can't believe it. She seemed like a lovely girl, James. I thought she looked so much like Brandy. Dad seemed so taken with her. So did Chelsea!"

"Everyone seemed to be taken in by her folksy ways, and I think that uncanny resemblance to Brandgwen made everyone let down their guard. Except me. I must say, I was never fooled. I knew there was something wrong about her. I watched her like a hawk."

"Thank you for taking such good care of my father," Jessie said with very real gratitude despite his snippy tone. James wasn't always the most likeable person, but his devotion to her father was beyond question.

"Oh." He was suddenly embarrassed. "My pleasure."

"James, I have to ask you something, and I know your first loyalty is to my father, but I am begging you to tell me what is going on there. Why won't he talk to me? Why hasn't he been returning my calls?"

James was silent for a moment. "He's not well, Jessica. He doesn't want you girls to know."

She had suspected something like that, and she could feel the tears smarting at her eyes.

"I'm coming home," she said.

"Please don't. Not tonight. I don't want him to guess I've told you. It wasn't my place. He's upset enough. Give it a few days, a week maybe. Then drop by *casually*."

She laughed despite her concern for her father. "Casually? It's hundreds of miles."

"In this family, that's casual. Ask Chelsea."

"He'll be okay? Until I get there?"

"He hasn't discussed his condition with me, but I am assuming he has months left. Perhaps a year."

Months? A year? Her beloved father?

Jessie hung up the phone. She was no longer engaged. Her father was ill, and it was not temporary.

She knew he was eighty-three. Knew she shouldn't feel so shocked, so amazed at the possibility she might lose him.

Look at him, even now, trying to protect his children from reality. Just as he had tried to protect them from the reality of who their mother was.

When Jessie thought of her father, she felt the most exquisite tenderness. She remembered him giving and giving and giving. She remembered how he had never seemed old, even though he had been close to sixty when she was born.

What had she ever given him in return? He was the man who had everything. She remembered how hard it had always been to shop for him for Father's Day, for his birthday, for Christmas gifts. She had always wanted to make the grand gesture, to find that one thing that would show him her love.

What would make him smile?

And in a sudden moment she knew what that could be.

She knew what she could give her father.

She calculated how quickly she could get at some of her assets. There were a lot of them. Her father had insisted on giving her an allowance all these years—she had been just as insistent on living on her income. Well, for the most part, anyway.

She could buy Jake the Silver Ghost. Was there an

irony that she would part with that money so willingly for him and had not once considered using it toward the house on the Hill that Mitch coveted?

She remembered she didn't have to worry about a house on the Hill with Mitch anymore.

What she did not expect was the flood of relief that filled her.

Garner Blake kept sliding looks at Jessie. He had always found her almost impossibly attractive, but after kissing her, he was finding it hard to be in the same room with her, something buzzing inside of him.

Today, sipping coffee at break, chatting with Ernie, teasing Clive, she looked like a different girl than the one who had covered his face with kisses in the hotel lobby last night.

She seemed somber. Was it regret?

"What happened to your ring?" Clive asked.

She looked down at her ring finger. There was only a faint white line where the ring had been.

How had Garner failed to notice that? And what the heck did it mean? Did it have something to do with the faint worry etched between her brows?

She was free! She had been dangerous enough before, but now—

"Oh," she said, and gave her hand a little shake. "I must have forgotten to put it on this morning."

What did he feel? Plenty. Intense regret mingled with relief. But when her eyes, green and deep, glanced off his, he knew it wasn't true. She hadn't forgotten that ring. She had taken it off her finger deliberately.

It was time to pull out of this. It really was. He was losing control of the situation. Losing control of himself. Because he wanted to push all these people out of the way and taste her lips again.

"Jessie." He cleared his throat. He was going to have to cancel the ride in the Silver Ghost. For his own self-preservation.

"Yes?"

He stared at her. Her lips were plump and sensuous. He remembered what they tasted like. He saw something like sadness flit through her eyes, and it felt as if it was his life's mission to chase that sadness away.

He was lost.

"I'll pick you up at seven," he said gruffly.

For a moment, the sadness was gone, and he wondered if she was going to push through all those guys and cover his face with kisses.

"Great," she said, and smiled. "I have a proposition for you."

He sighed. Propositioned by Jessica King. His life was spinning wildly, wildly out of control.

He hoped she was going to suggest naughty things in the backseat. A week ago, that would have been out of the question. But looking at her today, in those low-slung jeans and a tank top, he just wasn't so sure.

"Be still, my foolish heart," he muttered to himself.

It wasn't until he was in the safety of his office that a renegade thought blasted through his mind.

Was he falling in love with her?

His first answer was a vehement no. He knew better. They were from different worlds. There was bad blood between the families. She was educated, he wasn't. She had more money than Oprah; he was well-established, sure, but not in the same league as the King family.

But even while his rational mind was ticking off all

the reasons it wasn't possible, another part of him was ticking off another kind of checklist.

The way he felt inside, like the sun had come out in a world gone gray.

The way he liked being around her, just to see what she would say next.

The way his heart tumbled in his chest when he caught her scent or her gaze on him or the shine of her plump lips.

He put his head in his hands.

"Garner," he said softly, "you don't just have it, you have it bad."

And then he thought, *So what?* So what if he had it bad? He was nearly thirty years old. Maybe it was time for him to give love a chance. Maybe that was why, when he'd seen Clive's new pictures of the baby, he had felt things he'd never really felt before. A kind of melting sensation, as if there was nothing in the world he wanted more than that, to have a tiny human being relying on him to keep it safe, to love unconditionally, to be more of a man than he had ever been before.

Maybe that's why, last night, when he'd driven up to his house, with Jessie beside him, he'd been able to see a swing set in the backyard, hear the shouts of children as they leapt off that rope tied to the old willow.

Love had not been good to him. It had left him wary and battle-scarred, wearing armor. And in a single week, his armor was being dismantled, by her smile, by the light in those eyes, by her rich curves filling out a pair of blue jeans.

"That's not love," he told himself. "That's plain old lust."

But he could not convince himself that it was lust he had felt when he had finally taken her lips.

It had been so much more. A promise of a life he could not have imagined for himself, fuller and richer and deeper. He had not even known how lonely his life had become. He had not even known how empty he felt.

What did he have to show for his life? A fat bank account, a business, some beautiful cars. Suddenly that seemed like nothing compared to the riches she offered. Her eyes had promised him a life of laughter, of love, of the daily adventure of unraveling her many mysteries.

And today the ring was off her finger. She felt it, too! He knew she did. She wasn't the rich and spoiled women from his past. Jessie was not superficial, shallow or mean-spirited. His curse for finding exactly the wrong woman had been lifted.

Probably because he hadn't found her. She'd been sent to him.

He frowned. But not by heaven. By her father, Jake King, a sworn enemy of his family. He shook off the dark cloud that tried to block the sun of his happiness. He left work early to go make sure the car was in perfect order. He left early so that he could be what he had never been before with any other woman: utterly romantic.

So what kind of evening did you give a girl who had everything?

The Silver Ghost was a good start, but let's face it, she had been around the most exquisite cars in the world since before she was born. She had eaten in restaurants that were fancier than anything within a hundred miles of here. She certainly did not need him to buy her jewels or flowers.

So how did you declare yourself to a girl like that?

Declare himself? He ordered himself to put on the brakes. But instead, he recalled her face last night when she had watched the soap bubbles dance with the velvety darkness of night falling.

What did you give the girl who had everything?

He knew suddenly. You gave her all the things she'd never had—a chance to play Frisbee, an opportunity to drop a fishing pole into a secluded pond, an ice-cream soda at a drugstore fountain where absolutely no one knew who you were.

He had a lifetime of ordinary pleasures to give her, but that would make a good start for one evening. They'd drive over to the ice-cream parlor in Hollow Gap, play some Frisbee, end up back at his grandfather's pond.

He picked her up at the hotel. She looked adorable in denim capris, a scarf tied on her head. But her best fashion statement was the fact that the ring was still missing.

She handed him a paper bag.

"I had to think really hard," she said. "What do you get a guy who is taking you for a ride in a car like this?"

He laughed when he opened the bag. Champagne and two glasses. Very expensive champagne. The glasses didn't look cheap, either.

"I keep wondering when they're going to pop out with the camera," he said, "and tell me I'm on the latest reality show. *The Rich Girl and the Mechanic*."

"I don't think the average mechanic drives a car like this," she said as he held open the door for her.

That gave him a little pause. He was really just an average guy, in every way, except maybe the car, which he was going to have to sell sooner or later. Did she think he was something he was not? If she did, an hour of Frisbee should cure her of her illusions!

He took her hand before he started the car, looked at

the bare ring finger. "You didn't forget to put the ring back on, did you?"

"No," she said, and her voice was soft and tremulous.

"You ever played Frisbee?"

"What-bee?"

He laughed. They drove the car through town, and when people stopped and stared she waved at them. They all waved back, smiling.

"You know what?" she told him, laughing, wrinkling her nose at him. "I actually feel like a princess."

"Haven't you always?"

"I never have," she said.

He wanted to make her feel like the princess that she was. Maybe not everyone would have tried to accomplish that with a Frisbee, but he was a different kind of prince!

At the high school field, empty of children for the summer, he stopped, got out, fished his Frisbee out of the back of the car.

She was, as he had suspected she would be, hopeless at both Frisbee catching and throwing. Either that, or she liked the personalized instruction. Because he had to get right behind her, pull her in close to him, hold her arm and show her the proper fling movement. Soon she had him chasing that Frisbee all over the school yard. He had the pleased feeling she rather liked watching him run and make heroic leaps to catch her impossible offerings.

He finally collapsed.

"That was fun," she said, and came and sat in the grass beside him. He put his head on her lap, and looked up into the amazing green of her eyes.

"Is something bugging you?" he asked. "Is it about him?"

"Who?" she asked. Then, "Oh, Mitch. No, it's not

about that." Her hands found his hair, and absently she touched it, ran her hands through it.

"You aren't yourself," he decided.

"I found out some bad news last night, Garner."

He sat up. "What?"

"My dad's sick. I won't be able to stay. I'm going to go next week."

He felt a little sick himself. Go? But he still had so many things to show her.

"What's wrong with him?"

"I don't know. He didn't tell me. His personal assistant did. I'm hoping if I go home I'll be able to find out more."

"You were just getting the hang of the office, too." He said it to hide what he was really feeling.

"I'm sorry. I feel guilty about leaving you in the lurch. Could we not talk about it right now? I just want to enjoy every second you're willing to give me."

He leapt to his feet. Time for ice-cream sodas, then, before he did something really dumb and unmanly. Like begging her to stay. Like asking her how long she would be gone, or if she was coming back.

Or if a dumb mechanic figured into her plans for the future at all.

He drove to Hollow Gap, and they stopped at the old-fashioned ice-cream parlor. Nobody recognized her, though the car was causing quite a stir. But everything was different now. A pall had been cast over the evening. They tried to talk of small things—the weather, business, people gawking at the car—but he was too aware that everything had changed.

Nonetheless, he couldn't seem to abandon his original plan. He drove back to his grandfather's pond, and they sat in the very back seat, because it was elevated.

"I want to buy this car from you," she said. "That's the proposition I was talking about earlier."

He kept his voice carefully noncommittal. "Not exactly the proposition I was hoping for."

She rapped him playfully on the arm, as if she had no idea she was holding the hilt end of a knife that she'd buried in his heart.

"I want to buy it for my father."

Now there's *a surprise.*

"There's so little that he doesn't have. I feel like time is running out to show him how much I love him."

Then she was crying softly.

Crying! Sheesh. How was he supposed to handle that?

"I'll have to think about it," he said.

"You were selling it, weren't you? You said that's what you'd do with it eventually. The price doesn't matter. Whatever you want."

"Rich people," he said. "They always know the price of everything and the value of nothing."

"My father would know the value of this car."

"Whatever." He got out stiffly, just like a man who had been stabbed.

"I'll take you back to the hotel now."

"Garner, what's the matter?"

"That's why he sent you here. He wanted the car."

"He's never mentioned this car to me! I haven't even spoken to him since I got here."

"Yeah, whatever. Life is full of unbelievable coincidences. He calls one week and wants to buy the car. I tell him no. You show up. Now you want to buy the car. Only you played dirty."

"I didn't know he'd approached you about the car!"

He looked at her full in the face. Nobody could lie

that well. But it all boiled down to the same thing. Whatever trickery or wizardry or plain cunning Jake had used, the result was the same. It was about the car.

"What do you mean I played dirty?" she said, getting in the front seat, but squeezed over against the door, as far from him as she could get.

"You should have never involved personal feelings in it. That's dirty."

"You think I'm pretending to like you to get a car?" she asked, horrified.

He shrugged.

She got out of the car and slammed the door. Slammed it!

"Hey, watch the doors!"

"Watch them yourself," she said, and turned away.

"I'll drive you back to your hotel."

"I wouldn't get in that car with you if I was a thousand miles out in the desert and you came by and offered me a lift! How dare you question my integrity?"

"Oh, from the lady playing kissy-face with one guy while wearing another's ring."

He hadn't meant to hit her quite that hard. The anger drained from her face, and she looked momentarily shattered. Then she turned on her heel and walked away.

But Garner felt like the real heel was still sitting in his precious car.

Chapter Nine

Jessica King had never been so angry in her whole life. She would have liked to go back there and slam the car door until it fell off.

What a fool she had been! Thinking she was in love with Garner Blake! What a joke.

He was just like everyone else in her life. They appeared to be one thing, but they were really another.

Beginning with her mother, who had posed flawlessly as a devoted parent for the cameras, even though she had begun an affair with a gorgeous, unemployed actor only months after Jessie had been born. Even Mitch! He had appeared to be everything she ever wanted—stable and intellectual, established in a world far removed from the King millions! In the end he had been altered by her money. Suddenly he wanted a house on the Hill. When he'd popped the question, he wanted her to be different than she had always been—skinnier for one.

Jessie said a very bad word, very loudly, and kicked a rock so hard it hurt her toe. She felt instantly foolish and glanced around. But she seemed to have the streets of Farewell all to herself.

Then, in her peripheral vision, something moved.

Her heart climbed into her throat. Even though she had chosen the least public of roles of all the King children, she was still aware of who she was. That she could, at any time, because of her family's fame and her father's fortune, be a target for a nut case or a terrorist or a kidnapper.

Trying not to look as though she was looking, she glanced back.

It was Garner in the shadows.

Fresh fury boiled up in her.

For all that she realized, saying yes to Mitch had been a mistake. At least they had been civilized. They had never fought. The most squabbling they'd ever done had been in the past week!

She had a feeling with a man like Garner, there would be many fevered battles. He was stubborn and pig-headed. He'd want his own way all the time. He would have been an impossible man to share a life with. Thank goodness he'd forced her to her senses before she let drugging kisses decide the direction of the rest of her life!

Still, a small voice whined within her, making up after a battle with him would probably be as passionate as the battle itself.

The regret she felt was sharp, because of course she was never going to know that now.

He'd accused her of having an ulterior motive.

"Quit stalking me," she yelled at him. That was her, Jessica King, yelling like a fishwife on a public street! That's what passion got you!

"I'm not stalking you," he said with infuriating calm. "I'm making sure you get home safe."

"Well, don't. I'd rather be mugged." A mugger? In Farewell? She supposed such things happened. Just moments ago she had contemplated the vulnerability that came with a name like hers. Tonight would be a perfect night for a first encounter with a mugger. She'd love to have an innocent mugger to vent this rage on! She'd pummel him! She'd scratch his eyes out. She'd kick him where it counted.

She was surprised at herself, but not unpleasantly. She felt powerful in a way she was not sure she had ever felt before. She wanted to pick up one of those rocks she had been kicking and throw it right at Garner Blake's fat head!

She resisted that impulse, choosing to walk with regal pride down the darkening streets. She didn't acknowledge his presence again, but she could feel it in the shadows, bristling with energy as angry as her own. She arrived at the corner by her hotel, turned, meaning to dismiss him, to tell him haughtily to go home, a queen dismissing a servant. She was stunned when he was right behind her.

"How dare you creep up on me, like some kind of…creep!"

"I didn't creep up on you. Your brain is sizzling so loudly you didn't hear me."

She wanted to slap him. But that's not what she did. She wrapped her arms around him and pulled him into her. She stood on her tiptoes and took his lips. For a moment he was stiff with resistance, but then it melted and she felt, momentarily, the pleasure of the power born of pure passion.

He put his arms around her and dragged her tighter

to him. She could feel his sinewy strength and the strong beat of his heart. She could feel the blistering heat of his anger in the way his lips took hers. There was no tenderness in the exchange. It was punishing and primitive and strangely exhilarating, like walking way too close to an uncontrollable force.

He jerked away first, stared at her, his eyes gone black with passion and fury intertwined.

"Why did you do that?" he snapped finally, his voice hoarse.

"It was goodbye," she snapped back, her voice as hoarse with wanting as his.

He shoved his hands in his pockets, and she knew it was because if he didn't, he would grab her again. "Okay," he said. "Goodbye. And good riddance."

"Caveman," she said, wiping her lips with a great show of ferocious distaste.

"At least that's honest."

She glared at him and marched away before she gave in to the temptation to do it all over again!

She didn't know exactly what she had hoped to accomplish with that kiss, but she knew what she had accomplished. She was branded, his power and passion imprinted on her in some place that would make it impossible to taste another man without comparisons, without yearning for that kind of heat. It had been a predatory kiss. They'd laid claim to each other in some deeply primal way, even as they had said they didn't want each other.

She paused at the hotel door and took one last look over her shoulder. He was walking away, his hands shoved deep into his pockets. He gave a stone a kick that should have broken it in two.

"Good riddance, yourself," she muttered, and she was still angry enough to think she believed it.

Garner Blake had never been so angry. He was furious with himself for letting his guard down and with her for being everything he had always believed all women to be—manipulative and conniving.

Yet, still surprising.

Whew, the heat in that last kiss could have set the whole town on fire.

There were elements to Jessie he didn't know. That he was never going to know now.

He tried to tell himself he was relieved. He was glad it had all been about the car.

But he knew he was lying.

The next day at work, when she didn't come in, he said gruffly to the others that she didn't work there anymore. Clive glared at him.

"Whatcha gone and done to Jess?"

"She had to go home. Her dad's sick."

Clive looked at him and seemed to know there was a lot more to the story.

Garner braced himself for the lecture that didn't come.

Instead, Clive slammed him sympathetically on the back a couple times. "It'll work out, boss."

"What will work out?" he asked, his voice stiff with pride.

"Whatever's supposed to," Clive said, and then, uninvited, told Garner the whole story of the ugly fight he and his wife had before he'd asked her to marry him. Of course, it was no big secret. The whole town had talked about Clive climbing up on the old water tower and painting over the declaration of love he'd put up there just the week before.

"It's a roller-coaster ride," Clive finished sagely.

But Garner was aware his roller-coaster ride was over.

Yet it wasn't. Days passed. She was everywhere in his office now—her neat handwriting on this invoice, her notes on the desk, her quotes for jobs beginning to come in. He lay awake at night and felt the heat of that final savage kiss. In weak moments he relived the more tender one, on the tailgate of his truck.

Instead of his fury and confusion diminishing it seemed to be growing.

But it was not directed at Jessica.

It was directed at her father. How could Jake King have done that? How could he have used his daughter's charm in such a mercenary manner? How could he play with lives as if people were just lead soldiers lined up in front of him, waiting for him to move them this way and that?

Finally, Garner could not contain himself. When he could not find a business number, Garner had his lawyers find Jake's personal, well-guarded number.

The phone was answered by a snooty man. A personal assistant, Garner remembered Jessie had said. It was probably going to be harder to get through to Jake King than to the president of the United States. But he was surprised that when he gave his name he was put through instantly.

Of course, he had the trump card. He had that cursed car that Jake wanted.

"King here."

"Blake here."

Silence as they faced off.

Then Garner said what he least wanted to say. "Is Jessie okay?"

"No, she isn't." The answer was sharp enough that

Garner knew if they were face-to-face and Jake had a sword, he would run him through.

"What do you mean, she isn't?"

"She has this phony smile pasted to her face, and her eyes are all puffy."

It was everything Garner could do not to slam down the phone and grab the next plane. Her eyes were puffy? She was crying? He preferred to think of her steaming mad!

"I want you to know," Garner said, his voice stiff with dislike, "how little respect I have for a man who would use his own daughter the way you did."

Silence, and then Jake said, "Go on."

"You wanted the car. And you knew what would happen when she came here."

More silence.

"Everybody loves her. My mechanics. My customers. Even your aunt Hetta was taken with her. I'm sure you know Hetta hates everybody equally."

Silence.

"Even the damn pig loved her!"

Still that aggravating silence.

"So was that the game plan?" Garner asked, his voice strained. "Send her here to charm the socks off everybody and then have her ask for whatever she wanted? Whatever you wanted?"

"Everybody loved Jessie?"

Jake King sounded, well, stunned.

"You know what? You can have the damned car. I can't even look at it anymore without feeling sick."

"Everybody loved Jessie?" Jake repeated again.

"Yeah," Garner said, and he sounded defeated to his own ears. Everybody had loved her, especially him.

"Garner." Something had changed in that voice, and he noticed, with a bit of resentment, the switch from his last name to his first. "People don't react like that to Jessie."

"Excuse me?"

"They don't love her."

Garner wanted to jump right through the phone and strangle the old man for his blasphemy. What did he mean people didn't love Jessie? With the understandable exception of Fannie Klippenhopper, everybody loved her!

"Don't get me wrong," Jake said slowly. "Her family loves her. Her sisters and I would lay down our lives for her. But that's because with us, she could never hide who she truly is." He sighed.

"People don't like Jessie?" Garner asked and felt stricken for her.

"For the most part, people find Jessie aloof and disconnected. Intellectually snobby."

"*My* Jessie?" he said, and was sorry the minute the words popped out. Jessie was not his!

"Your Jessie," Jake said, picking up on it. But his voice held no malice.

"I didn't mean that the way it sounded."

"We need to talk," Jake said abruptly. "I'll send you a plane ticket."

"Keep your damn plane ticket. I can find you myself."

He slammed down the phone.

But he knew there was someone he had to see before he saw Jake and before he saw Jessica again.

He found his father, alone, on the back deck of the house Garner had bought him. It faced the twelfth hole of the Farewell Golf and Country Club.

"Garner," his father said. "How's the business?"

His father was always interested in the business that he'd done his damnedest to ruin.

"It's fine, Dad."

"Have you found a replacement for your aunt yet?"

"Um, wanted to talk to you about that."

He told him about Jake's interest in the car, about Jessica's arrival. He didn't mention anything about embarrassingly hard-to-control feelings or stealing savage kisses under streetlights.

"So does he own part of the business?" Garner asked. "What kind of mess am I in here?"

He was aware of feeling weary. He loved his father and was loyal to him, but oh, how weary he was of cleaning up messes he had not made.

Not that that could be said of the situation with Jessie.

That situation was one hundred percent his making—and he'd gone into it with his eyes wide-open, knowing damn well the situation needed to be handled with kid gloves and taking off the gloves anyway.

"The way I see it," his father said, lighting a cigar and putting his feet up on the balcony railing, "you aren't in any kind of mess at all, Garner."

"Well, I might be. He owns half the business. I don't exactly know what that means, and the lawyers are having trouble figuring it out, but now he's mad. He could pull the rug right out from under me."

"Garner, you're looking at this all wrong."

Garner waited, but he could feel a familiar dread unfolding in his stomach.

His father had a certain glitter in his eyes when he had a scheme.

"Is this the girl you followed home last night?

Were shouting at in the streets? Kissed in front of the hotel?"

Garner nodded reluctantly. Farewell was a small town. His father probably knew about those things before Jessie had even found the safety of her room.

"The same one you've been gallivanting around with in the Silver Ghost?"

Sometimes he hated small towns.

"You could have it all, Garner," his father said softly.

"What?"

"You could have what was rightfully yours to begin with. If you play your cards right with that girl, you could win back your family's share to Auto Kingdom."

Garner was silent. He looked at his father and he thought, sadly, how some things never changed.

"I don't want a share of Auto Kingdom," he said. "I'm happy with my own business."

"You and your grandfather." His father shook his head. "Neither of you ever had what it took to go after what's rightfully yours."

Garner suddenly saw what it took: a deep cynicism toward life, an ability to use, a hard-heartedness that bordered on ruthlessness, a total lack of integrity or empathy for other people.

Suddenly he understood where his own lack of trust came from.

His father was not an honorable man. And Garner was as afraid that his father resided in him as Jessica was afraid that her mother resided within her.

But sitting there with his father, he realized it was not true. He could not use Jessica. Or anyone else. It was not in him.

He had spent his life being attracted to women like

his mother, who wanted that ruthless quality in a man. Finally he had found a woman who didn't, and he had intentionally let something small get big, let his own pigheadedness get in the way of truth. He had wanted to misunderstand her desire for the car, he had wanted to find fault. He had wanted to fight with her. So that he wouldn't have to be vulnerable. Wouldn't have to say that frightening yes to love.

He'd let her go.

Why? So that one day, he could sit in a place like this, like his father, surrounded by luxuries, but all alone? As poor—as spiritually and emotionally bankrupt—as a man could ever be?

Now she was wandering around her father's estate. Puffy-eyed and fake-smiling.

Jessica might have been a pawn in her father's game, but Garner acknowledged the truth about her—a truth he had known in his heart since the minute she'd walked through the door and brightened the darkness of a life gone too lonely.

She was not capable of using someone to reach her own ends.

He had to get to her before she put that horrible ring back on her finger.

He sprang up so quickly, he nearly knocked over the chair.

"Where you going in such a fired-up rush, son?"

"I'm going to get her."

"That's my boy," his father said.

But Garner knew, with a relief so great it set his heart free, that he was nothing like his father. Maybe love could work for him.

* * *

The next day he was ushered straight into Jake's office. He had thought Jake might make him endure a humiliating wait, but it wasn't that way.

He'd also thought he might be intimidated by Kingsway, but the thing that interested him most about the estate was that Jessie was here. It wouldn't be that easy to find her in this place if she didn't want to be found.

He looked at the place not as an overly awed boy who'd grown up poor, but as a girl who'd grown up rich. For all its treasures, Kingsway seemed empty of the kinds of things Jessie might have liked and needed. Frisbees, fishing poles and bubbles, just to begin with.

Garner had met Jake only once before, though he'd seen many pictures of him in automotive publications. He knew right away that the illness was real. Jake looked frail. But his handshake was firm and so was his voice.

"I brought you the car," he told Jake. "I want to trade it."

"You think I'd trade you a car for my daughter?" Jake asked, incensed.

"Don't be ridiculous. What's between your daughter and me is between your daughter and me. She's a grown woman and free to make her own choices."

Jake settled back, and Garner bore his scrutiny. He was surprised by a hint of a smile. "What do you want for the car then?"

"Free title to my business and the property it sits on."

Jake nodded. "Done."

"So you got what you wanted. Where's Jessica?"

Jake chortled harshly. "You foolish young pup."

Garner stiffened.

"Look at me. You think I got what I wanted? What good is a car going to do me where I'm going? Do you really think it was ever about the car?"

Garner stared at him.

"A long, long time ago, I had a friend. We grew up together. We explored every mountain trail together. We pooled our money and bought our first car together. We fished every stream and pond in Virginia and West."

"My grandfather," Garner said.

"I loved him like a brother. I guess what I'm saying, if you can hear me, is that a long time ago there was a place I belonged. When a man reaches the end of his life as I am, he realizes what is important. He hopes the best things can survive. "

Garner said slowly, "I'm not sure I'm following you."

Jake said, his voice so soft that Garner had to strain to hear it, "I didn't send her there to manipulate you out of your car. I sent her there hoping she would find herself and find where she belongs."

Garner spoke, his voice sharp with cynicism. "How could you know she'd find that in Farewell? With me?"

"I didn't. But hope is a powerful thing. I hoped good things for her. Every man hopes that for his children. Then I saw her getting more and more lost in that university world of hers. And that man…" Jake shook his head empathetically.

He was silent for a minute, and then seemed to gather strength. "When you told me that people there loved her, I knew she was finally on her way to finding where she belonged. Though, I'll admit when I saw your picture on the Internet, so like your grandfather, I hoped the best thing about Simon and I would survive after all."

"And that was?"

Jake smiled. "It was love, of course. I hoped the love would survive."

"You were matchmaking?" Garner asked, outraged. "You sent your daughter to Farewell hoping there might be a future for us? For me and Jessie?"

"The future Simon and I threw away. I suppose that makes me a scheming old bastard." He said this without one iota of apology.

"I suppose it does," Garner said, but without heat. After a long moment, he extended his hand.

Jake took it. The handshake was firm. Their eyes met.

Garner felt grateful to the old man for not saying a single word about his father's dishonesty, excesses or mismanagement.

"About the car..." Jake said.

"I'll sign it over to you today."

Jake nodded. "You understand I won't be needing it for very long."

He looked at the old man, and he did understand. He was putting his affairs—all of them—in order.

"Yeah," he said gruffly, "I understand that."

"Perhaps you know of a charity that would benefit from that car when I don't need it anymore."

"Farewell desperately needs a Boys & Girls Club. The sale of a car like that could give them a good start."

"Done," Jake said.

Garner reluctantly realized he could like this man very much. And what was so bad about that? He was going to be his father-in-law, after all.

That was, if he could talk Jake's pigheaded daughter into saying yes.

Chapter Ten

Jessie King peered out the window of the apartment above her father's garage where she had been making herself at home for the past few days.

She gasped and let the curtain fall, picked it up again and looked out to make sure she was not dreaming.

Garner's Silver Ghost was parked in the courtyard.

Of course, it might not be Garner's. He had told her that her father was looking for a car like that one. When Garner had refused to sell it, had her father found another one? Really, Jake King was rich enough to buy anything he wanted. He didn't need Garner's car. She should have pointed that out to Garner when she had the opportunity. Of course, *now* she had about a million things she wanted to say to him. And none of them were nice.

Since returning, she had not mentioned Garner, the car, Farewell, Virginia, or K & B Auto to her father. She had been shocked by how ill he looked, and she didn't want him taking on her troubles or revisiting his old ones. No, she played chess with him and looked through old photos and relived fond memories and smiled, smiled, smiled. Sometimes she would catch him studying her, as if he wasn't the least bit fooled by her smiles, but she just smiled harder.

How many Rolls-Royce Silver Ghosts were there? How many of them had black and burgundy exteriors, cream leather interiors and ragtops?

Her heart told her not that many. Her heart told her Garner had come to Kingsway and not about the car, either.

He had come for her, like a warrior come to claim his princess bride.

That was pretty fanciful thinking for the pragmatic one, Jessie scolded herself. Still, her stomach did a twist that would have put a roller coaster to shame. Somehow all those *nasty* things she wanted to say were disappearing from her mind.

She let the curtain drop again and realized, if he had come for her, she was in big trouble. Princess, indeed. She was a mess! She was in the most horrible outfit that she had donned for mourning days ago. It was a pair of gray oversize sweatpants, with a top that matched perfectly in poor fit and ugliness. Though she reluctantly changed out of the sweats when she spent time with her father, she hadn't washed her hair or put on makeup since she'd arrived home.

That was after she'd made the most terrible discovery. Try as she might, she couldn't even eat her sadness away. Chocolate, which had always provided her great solace in life's trying moments, tasted like sawdust. She'd had some flown in from Belgium, but it was no better than the barely touched box of Godiva by her bedside table. She'd sent one of the staff all the way to New York to bring her back a Serendipity frozen hot chocolate. The normally heavenly treat had tasted like swill.

Obviously, her taste buds were as broken as her heart. She had given up trying to eat her heartbreak away and tried to watch soap operas instead. Mitch didn't approve of soap operas, which she thought would have made her feel a teensy bit gleeful when indulging in them, but it soon became apparent to her that Mitch's opinion, which had mattered so much to her for so long, just didn't matter anymore. She felt no glee, and no respite from the empty feeling in the vicinity of her heart. Try as desperately as she might to lose herself in the complicated twists of the lives of the people in the stories, it simply didn't work. The programs could not hold her attention. And neither could books of any kind—romance, biology, history. She could not focus. Instead the words would blur and she would hear, in her mind, a bold laugh, or see, in her mind, dark eyes. Or feel, to the soles of her feet, the way she felt when sensuous lips had captured hers.

The only thing that had brought her even the slightest amount of solace from the overpowering sensation of loss was over there on that table by the window. Her laptop showed Garner Blake's Web page. She had looked obsessively at every car he had ever rebuilt, at every picture of him. It was pathetic, and she knew it, and she was so grateful that the Web page existed so that she could indulge in the guilty pleasure of seeing him.

A knock came at the door. It wasn't the hesitant tap of one of the servants bringing her a tray of food that she would return uneaten. No, it was a powerful hammering, insistent, undeniably masculine. Her heart began to race unreasonably.

"Who is it?" she called after a moment. Was her voice shaking?

"You know damn well who it is. You've been peeking out at that car since I arrived."

"I have not!" she said, and the quake in her voice disappeared.

"Open the door."

She'd forgotten, while she was mooning over his pictures, how bossy and autocratic Garner Blake could be! There was no sense him thinking he was ever going to have the upper hand with her! There was no sense him knowing how happy she was to hear his voice, the joy bounding within her like a hound after a rabbit.

Besides, if she opened that door too quickly, he might guess she'd been mooning over him, fretting about the direction of love and of life. And that wouldn't do!

"I'm not opening the door," she said.

"Yes, you are. If we're going to fight, we're going to do it face-to-face."

She looked down at her sweat suit, touched a lock of hair that felt distinctly greasy.

"We're not going to fight. I'm not opening the door."

"Open it or I'll break it down, so help me, Jessie."

She felt a shiver of pure appreciation at his masculine impatience.

"Caveman," she said.

"Hmm. I think that's where we left off."

Suddenly, she didn't want to play anymore. She just wanted to see him, to forgive him, to hold him, to kiss him. But not looking like this! She was going to tell him to come back in an hour, but before she could, there was an enormous crack. The wood around the frame of the door splintered and then the door flew open. He stood there, looking quite satisfied with himself, his hands folded over the broadness of his chest. He didn't exactly look like a man who had come begging for forgiveness.

Some men might have dressed up to come to Kingsway, but she was so pleased that he hadn't. She looked at the curve of his bicep under the hem of his T-shirt, and then into the flashing darkness of his eyes. She licked her lips.

Despite the confidence of that stance, did he look just a little bit worried? As if he wasn't quite certain of the reception he would receive?

"Hello, Jessie," he said casually, as if he had not just broken down her door.

She looked at him like a thirsty person catching their first glimpse of an oasis, as if he, and he alone, could save her from the desert that her life had been before he came, and would be again if he ever left her.

"I came to beg for your forgiveness," he said, his voice low. "I accused you of using me to get at that car, and I know now that I was one hundred percent wrong and that my saying something like that says a whole lot more about me than about you."

She looked at him and saw his utter sincerity. How could a man like this love her?

Yet that was what she saw in his eyes.

Love.

Garner Blake loved her. There was helplessness and tenderness and just a touch of terror in his eyes as he looked at her.

Her heart swelled and swooped like a bird celebrating the wind.

The game was up.

She ran to him.

"Thank you," he said. He took her to him, held her tight, lifted her face and covered it with kisses. Finally, a little bit breathless, he put her away from him and studied her.

Insecurity clawed at her. She was a mess. He was going to wonder why he had come so far, for this.

He scowled. "Have you been losing weight?"

"Maybe a little." That's what he noticed? Not the sweat suit, or the hair, or the lack of makeup?

"I bet there's someplace around here where we could find a great ice-cream soda," he said, and he touched her face, his fingertips tracing lines where tears had fallen, with regret and with healing.

"I bet there is," she said, smiling. The future she had been fretting about held this wonderful, funny, handsome, sensitive man. And not a Slim Gym in sight!

"I need to shower," she stammered. "I need to fix my hair, change clothes."

He looked at her quizzically, as if he was just noticing her hair and the horrible sweat suit. "Tell you what. I'll go pick up some ice cream and come back. We need privacy for what I want to say to you."

She felt a shiver begin at her toes and travel all the way to her ears. She turned from him quickly, before the urge to kiss him some more took over, and dashed for the bathroom. She heard him go out the broken door. He didn't try to shut it behind him.

A little later, in a shirt that said Farewell Forever, and jeans, she heard him come back in. Then she heard him humming. She peeked out the bathroom door.

Garner was in the tiny kitchen. He looked so comfortable rummaging through her cupboards. He found two large glasses and scooped ice cream and poured root beer.

Other men might have brought champagne.

But he was not like other men.

He had always had a gift for making the ordinary seem extraordinary.

Watching him in her kitchen, his back to her, the simple play of muscle, his comfort with himself, she knew that her future held this, small moments one after another, made perfect not by what was going on, but the love that infused those moments. That's what it was all about. It wasn't about glorious, but fleeting moments. It was about finding glory in the smallest of things.

Once she had daydreamed about a wedding, with her in a flowing gown designed for her by Dior. She had imagined herself carrying French Lace floribunda roses, flown in from Oregon, walking gracefully down the aisle of a huge cathedral. She had imagined the groom turning to look at her, but she realized she had never imagined his face.

Now she could see his face very, very clearly, and the rest of her vision evaporated before the power and purity of what she saw.

Before, it was as if the wedding had mattered more than the marriage—as if that one glorious moment would matter more than all the ones that followed.

"The ice cream is melting."

Ones just like this one—when a man glanced over his shoulder at you and the look in his eyes wove gold threads into the most ordinary of moments—that was what mattered and what sustained through other times. Times of hardship and sickness, heartbreak and loss, times that every life held.

"Come on," he said. "I can't propose to you over melted ice cream."

She slipped out of the bathroom, even though her hair was not perfect and she had no makeup on.

He didn't even know.

He had no idea she was not perfect, just the way she was.

He held out her ice cream to her and led the way to the sofa. He plopped down beside her, comfortable, and waved his spoon at her. "I saw what you were looking at on the Internet," he said.

"Oh!" The soda tasted rich and creamy, like clouds mixed with cream. Then playfully, she flung a little bit of ice cream off the tip of her spoon. It landed on his cheek, and he scooped it with his finger, put it in his mouth.

Her eyes fastened on his lips and on that finger.

"Don't get the idea I'm obsessed with you," she said hoarsely.

"No? You were on my Web site why?"

"Because I like old cars."

"Tut-tut. Honesty, Jessie."

Suddenly that's what she wanted more than anything in the world. Honesty. A place where she could be who she was and say what she wanted. A place where there were no games, no manipulation, no unspoken rules, no hidden truths.

"Okay," she admitted. "I was looking at you."

He wagged his eyebrows at her, took a big bite of ice cream, did some criminal things with his tongue on the spoon. "And?"

She swallowed hard. "I particularly like the picture of you leaning over the engine of the Silver Ghost."

"Why?"

Have mercy! "You have a nice butt." She blushed.

"I don't know if I'm going to be able to handle honesty from you, Jessie."

She set down her ice cream.

"You have a little something right there," she said, leaning toward him, pressing her leg against his.

"Where?" His voice was a tormented growl.

She touched the corner of his lip with her fingertip, ever so lightly. And then she leaned even closer, so close that she could feel her heartbeat synchronizing with his. She took the ice cream from his lip with a quick dart of her tongue.

"I've wanted to do that all of my life," she said. "Only, I didn't know it until I met you. I wanted to blow bubbles and play Frisbee and dangle my feet over a pond on a hot summer afternoon." She traced his lips with her fingers. "And I've wanted to do this." She kissed his ears. "And this. How am I doing in the honesty department so far?"

"Jessie, you better let me say what I have to say before the words slip away,"

She went very still. She moved away from him, but with effort.

He set down his ice cream. He slipped off the couch and got down on one knee. She had never seen a sight quite as moving as that—this big, self-possessed strong man, on one knee before *her*. The pudgy princess. The pragmatic one. The brainy one.

"I think I loved you from the first moment that you crashed your car into the meter outside K & B," he said softly, his eyes locked on hers. "From the first dab of chocolate I cleaned from your face."

"Garner, you're going to make me cry," she whispered.

"So cry," he said. "I'm only doing this once in my whole life, so I'm doing it right."

The tears started.

"When I look at you," he said softly, "I think of the future in new ways. I think of taking cross-country trips in an old car. I think of picnics by the pond. I think of putting up a picket fence and fixing the shutters."

His voice softened and he went on. "I think of nights with you in my arms and of chubby babies and of teaching a little boy how to throw a fly-fishing line.

"I think of sneaking up behind you and rubbing the tension out of your shoulder when you're all hunched over a book, studying for your doctorate.

"I think I've been so lonely, and you were brought to me, like an angel, to take that loneliness away."

He reached into his shirt pocket, took out a box and opened it.

A ring winked at her.

The most beautiful ring she had ever seen, small and delicate, the lines simple and tasteful. He slid it onto her finger, and she looked at it. It looked as if it had been made for her hand. It felt right in a way that other ring she had worn never, ever had.

"Will you marry me?" His voice was so gruff, so sweet, so full of yearning and promise.

"Yes," she whispered.

"You have a little bit of ice cream right there." He touched the corner of her lip with his finger.

"I know," she said.

He kissed it off.

"I did that on purpose," she admitted.

"I know," he said.

They laughed until they could laugh no more. And

what they didn't know was that their laughter floated out through the open window and filled the air with music. What they didn't know was that Jake King was out in the courtyard inspecting his new car. He could hear his daughter and Garner Blake laughing, and he closed his eyes in gratitude, for he knew he had asked a great deal of the universe, and he knew he was probably unworthy of receiving what he had asked for. Yet he was receiving it anyway.

He opened his eyes and looked at the sky, at the clouds drifting, at the intense bright blue, and for a moment he felt as if he had been lifted so high on the wings of love that he was part of that sky, touching it, breathing it, becoming it. He was aware that, until that moment, he had been pretending he was not afraid to die, but that he really had been. Now that fear was lifted from him.

The laughter rippled out across the courtyard again, his beautiful, somber child happy at last, everything in this great and wonderful world exactly as it was meant to be.

Epilogue

Chelsea King was teed off. She knew it was wrong to feel that way at her own sister's wedding, but she couldn't help it.

What was Jessica thinking? A backyard wedding for a King princess? In Farewell, Virginia, a town so obscure that it had no airport, no shopping center and only one hotel! With no room service! It didn't even provide the nice thick terry robes Chelsea liked. There had certainly not been a chocolate on her pillow last night when she had finally gone to sleep.

To make matters worse, the backyard was located behind a house that was so old Chelsea considered it spooky. The chairs looked as if they had been borrowed from the local community hall and were set up around a pond that was pretty enough in a rustic way, but that Chelsea was convinced was producing mosquitoes. She had been bitten twice.

What had Jessie been thinking? And what was the rush?

Chelsea didn't want another one of her sisters getting married. It felt so much less like they belonged to her!

She had met Garner briefly last night. He was so handsome it made her teeth hurt. And the way he had looked at her sister had made it very apparent who Jessie belonged to now.

Chelsea's whole life felt as if it was in an uproar. She was aware of feeling mad at the world. The feeling had started when she'd found out Sarah—someone she'd befriended and felt unusually close to—had tried to steal from her father. Then she'd disappeared without saying goodbye. Okay, so you didn't stick around to say a formal goodbye after you'd been caught filling your bags with other people's stuff, but even so!

Chelsea glared over at Cameron McPherson. She'd always thought Cameron was okay, but she didn't anymore. She wasn't sure if she hated him, yet, but it might be coming. Which was wrong, because she was probably related to him because her sister was married to his brother.

Chelsea had shown up just as he was going through Sarah's apartment. He said things weren't adding up. If Sarah wanted to steal things, Cameron had asked out loud, the apartment was loaded. Why hadn't she just taken stuff from there? There were valuable old paintings, crystal, a pretty good stereo and TV set. But frankly, Chelsea didn't want to hear him making excuses.

Lots of things weren't adding up for her, either. They'd been friends. If Sarah had needed money so desperately, why hadn't she just asked for it? And why had Sarah acted almost snootily proud when Chelsea gave her things, if she was going to turn around and steal whatever she wanted, anyway?

Thinking about the whole situation just gave Chelsea a headache, so she tried not to think about it. Then, without warning, there had been another upset in her life. The man who had acted as Chelsea's security practically since she was a baby had announced he was retiring. Chelsea knew Winslow was old—at least fifty—but retire? Chelsea felt nearly as betrayed by his retirement as by Sarah's treachery. Had it been just a job? Didn't he really care about her? He hadn't said a proper goodbye, either. He'd phoned her and said he was leaving, and that was that.

Now Cameron had personally taken over her security until he hired a replacement. She was finding him quite a bit bossier and more domineering than poor Winslow had ever been. He also was not nearly as good at fading into the woodwork. People noticed Cameron. It was pretty hard not to. He was about six feet of gorgeous male.

She'd actually flirted with him a bit, in a bored moment, and he hadn't even noticed. He was so focused on stupid Sarah. They'd driven to Farewell together, something she had never done with Winslow, but how could she say she didn't travel with the help when they were sort of related?

He'd spoiled the whole trip by grilling her about Sarah, which had made her realize how remarkably little she did know. He'd told her he'd found out Sarah was from a little town called Hollow Gap, just a few miles from Farewell.

Did she think that was strange? Did she mind if they stopped there on the way home so he could ask a few questions?

She didn't think it was that strange, and she wished he wouldn't talk about it. She certainly didn't want to stop in any place called Hollow Gap!

When Chelsea had changed the subject, and asked him when they were going to start interviewing a replacement for Winslow, he'd told her, as if she were a child, that she wasn't interviewing anyone. That he had someone in mind.

And then he hadn't let her bring any of her friends with her to this stupid wedding, because Jessie wanted it private and all her friends were too high-profile.

A woman came and sat down beside Chelsea.

She introduced herself. "Hetta King."

She looked old and wrinkled and her suit, though obviously well cut, smelled of mothballs. It was evident she was *eccentric* even without her saying a word.

She smiled politely.

"I hope this is fast," Hetta said.

At least they had that in common.

"I had to leave Benjamin Franklin at home."

Chelsea didn't ask. She already knew. Benjamin Franklin was probably an aging husband or mangy old cat, and nothing interested her less than hearing details about either. She smiled politely again, and then looked to the mountains.

She inadvertently shivered. They seemed dark and forbidding and too full of mysteries. She glanced around for her father.

He was standing behind the chairs waiting for Jessica's grand arrival so he could escort her up the aisle.

Another thing changing. Did people think she was so self-involved she couldn't tell he wasn't feeling well? Her stomach did a horrible dip at the thought.

She saw that he, too, was looking at the mountains. He was like a man looking at a work of art that he loved. He seemed as if he could look at those mountains all day and never get enough. As if his soul was filling up, as if this was his home and he had finally made his way back.

Imagine liking this place better than Kingsway!

He looked at her suddenly, as if he had sensed her watching him. She knew he wanted her to see what he saw, to feel it, but she couldn't. She looked at her watch instead, glanced up to see the disappointment cross his face, before he looked away again, to the mountaintops.

She always disappointed him. She suspected he found her too much like the mother she had never known, but heard plenty about over the years.

The wedding march began finally. Chelsea turned toward the music.

An old rattletrap of a truck was trundling along a road leading down to the chairs and the pond. When it came to an arc of trees, bubbles blew around it.

That was a nice touch, she decided reluctantly.

The truck stopped where her father was waiting and he opened the vehicle's door.

Chelsea steeled herself.

Jessica had refused her help last night. Wouldn't even let her have a peek at the dress. Jessica could not be trusted with matters of high fashion.

Wedding disaster about to happen, Chelsea narrated silently.

And it did.

Jessie stepped from the truck.

No! Her sister was wearing blue jeans. And a navy blue T-shirt. She had a veil tacked to her head with what appeared to be a child's tiara.

Chelsea started to close her eyes and moan, but something stopped her and made her look more closely at her sister. She felt her eyes film with tears.

She had never seen Jessica look like that—so radiant, so utterly joyous, so carefree.

Her uptight sister took her father's arm with relaxed confidence. She smiled at the guests, blew a kiss to Brandy and then waved at Chelsea.

Chelsea felt ridiculously honored to have been singled out by this beautiful woman.

Jessica and her father moved down the makeshift aisle between the chairs.

Chelsea could barely breathe. There was a light pouring out of her sister that was unearthly. That erased, instantly, the gloom of the mountains, the sting of her anger at Sarah, her discomfort over the mosquitoes, her feeling slighted that she had not been asked to help with hair and makeup, that there were no bridesmaids.

Chelsea realized she was looking at pure love.

Jessie's groom had appeared now beneath the willow, and he waited. A gorgeous man, he easily could have been a movie star or a model or a prince. And that same light—powerful, healing, amazing—poured from him as he looked at Jessie.

For the first time in Chelsea's memory her sister looked the part she had been assigned by America's adoring public. In her blue jeans and T-shirt, with a child's toy tiara clamped to her blond curls, Jessica was a princess.

A strange and lovely feeling filled Chelsea as she watched Jessie reach for the hand of the man she would marry and let go of the hand of her father. It was a feeling of time moving, flowing like a river, a child becoming a woman, a princess becoming a queen, all of life changing. She recognized the feeling as hope: Change was not necessarily a bad thing; love could be as real as it felt in this moment.

Someday it would find her as it had found her sisters.

She sighed and closed her eyes. She realized she was crying and thanked her lucky stars the press had not caught a whiff of this event, because there was truly no such thing as tear-proof mascara. When she opened her eyes again, it was as if the light had changed. Everything, even those mountains drenched in the gold of love. And made different by it.

Even her.

* * * * *

Don't miss Chelsea's story!
PRICELESS GIFTS (RS #1822)
Available July 2006!

If you enjoyed what you just read,
then we've got an offer you can't resist!

Take 2 bestselling love stories FREE!

Plus get a FREE surprise gift!

Clip this page and mail it to Silhouette Reader Service™

IN U.S.A.	IN CANADA
3010 Walden Ave.	P.O. Box 609
P.O. Box 1867	Fort Erie, Ontario
Buffalo, N.Y. 14240-1867	L2A 5X3

YES! Please send me 2 free Silhouette Romance® novels and my free surprise gift. After receiving them, if I don't wish to receive anymore, I can return the shipping statement marked cancel. If I don't cancel, I will receive 4 brand-new novels every month, before they're available in stores! In the U.S.A., bill me at the bargain price of $3.57 plus 25¢ shipping and handling per book and applicable sales tax, if any*. In Canada, bill me at the bargain price of $4.05 plus 25¢ shipping and handling per book and applicable taxes**. That's the complete price and a savings of at least 10% off the cover prices—what a great deal! I understand that accepting the 2 free books and gift places me under no obligation ever to buy any books. I can always return a shipment and cancel at any time. Even if I never buy another book from Silhouette, the 2 free books and gift are mine to keep forever.

210 SDN DZ7L
310 SDN DZ7M

Name	(PLEASE PRINT)	
Address	Apt.#	
City	State/Prov.	Zip/Postal Code

Not valid to current Silhouette Romance® subscribers.

Want to try two free books from another series?
Call 1-800-873-8635 or visit www.morefreebooks.com.

* Terms and prices subject to change without notice. Sales tax applicable in N.Y.
** Canadian residents will be charged applicable provincial taxes and GST.
All orders subject to approval. Offer limited to one per household.
® are registered trademarks owned and used by the trademark owner and or its licensee.

SROM04R   ©2004 Harlequin Enterprises Limited

HOTEL MARCHAND

**Four sisters.
A family legacy.
And someone is out to destroy it.**

A captivating new limited continuity, launching June 2006

The most beautiful hotel in New Orleans,
and someone is out to destroy it. But mystery,
danger and some surprising family revelations
and discoveries won't stop the Marchand sisters
from protecting their birthright…
and finding love along the way.